Three Women,

Two Days,

and a Night.

By:

Jude Lawson

Three Women, Two Days, and a Night

Copyright © 2016 by Jude Lawson

ISBN: 978-0-9975505-1-1

First Electronic Edition: May 2016

Pagoda Publishing, Crestwood, KY 40014

Dedication

A wise woman once said,

"The women in the world who seek to find the mystery

and romance in love are the greatest of all."

I dedicate my book to those great women.

Table of Contents

Table of Contents

Prologue

The sun radiates down upon all those walking in
the masses of the street in front of The Little Columbian
Coffee Shoppe. The occasional soft summer breeze
creating the ideal day for all those venturing outside. The
air is electric as the day begins anew on this warm summer
day. A few wisps of clouds, with the wonderful weather
woman threatening rain for the following afternoon, has
not stopped anyone from dawning their summer best. Be
it skimpy outfits for the day off or sleek light dresses for

work, a quarter of the midsized town is enjoying the beautiful morning.

A brunette haired woman walks out of the coffee shop, stopping on the edge of the sidewalk. She takes a sip of her mochaccino and squints upwards at the sun bouncing off the few surrounding sky scrapers a block away from the shop. She takes one step closer to the curb just as a red headed woman coming from across the street tries to slip past her to avoid a bike messenger whipping by with little regard to the pedestrians and motorists.

"Ow," The brunette haired woman switches the hand holding the mochaccino as hot liquid spills on her thumb and down the back of her now free hand.

"Sorry, the bike messenger came faster than I thought he would," The redhead watches as the brunette haired woman shakes the hot liquid from her burning hand.

The brunette haired woman curls one side of her

mouth in a sexual mannerism, "It's not a big deal. Happens from time to time on my own. Even this can't ruin today."

A blonde stands just to the side of the coffee shop door watching the two women interact. She notices, despite the intense heat, the red head has on all black. She has on a cross between skimpy sexy and Goth clothing. The brunette haired woman gives the typical slutty secretary style appearance. The blonde watches as the two women turn to go their separate ways.

Chapter One

The smell of strawberries and melons blows on a

soft summer breeze as the blonde woman turns towards

the glass coffee shop door allowing her long hair to scent

the wind. She reaches out her left hand grabbing the

door's large rectangular metal handle on the right side of

the steel frame. She looks down at an empty coffee cup as

it slowly rolls past the door from the breeze. She leans

back slightly pulling on the door. The heavy setting of the

hydraulic arm on the top of the door makes it hard for her

to pull open. Not surprising when the little lady is only

weighing one hundred and twenty five pounds.

The door begins to close slowly as she steps inside. The door chime sounds as she crosses the laser detector at the base of the door frame hidden by two unrealistic fake plants of some unknown species. She looks around at the people sitting in the coffee shop enjoying their fresh morning brew. She lowers her head slightly walking to the front counter as if everyone else is also paying attention to her the way she notices them. She watches as the slightly plump barista wipes off the counter with a damp cloth. The barista drops the dirty cloth into a soapy water bucket at the end of the counter drying her hands on the green apron around her waist.

"Hello Abigail," the barista, of average height, turns to the young blonde woman, "Do you want the usual or are you finally going to try something new?"

Abigail smiles sheepishly at the twenty four year old brunette behind the counter, "No Tonya, just the usual for me. I don't think I can chance a problem with the studying I have to do for next week."

Tonya looks the skinny blonde up and down observing her typical conservative clothing, "I forgot you have finals next week for your summer classes. Think you're going to do okay?"

Tonya turns and begins to fix the amaretto cream latte while listening to Abigail, "Yeah, I thought it would be good to get a little ahead in school. But, now I'm not so sure. I don't feel ready for the summer classes and I am having trouble relaxing so I can focus on my work."

"You have always been and always will be a straight 'A' student," Tonya leans towards Abigail pushing the finished latte across the counter and lowering her voice to a whisper, "Maybe my innocent little bookworm just needs to get laid."

Abigail looks down at the latte as her face turns bright red, "I haven't found the right guy. And, I don't know that I am ready for that. Besides, I have never had a guy look at me twice, so I doubt it could happen anyways."

Tonya stands up straight smiling without altering the volume of her voice, "No problem. You are a skinny girl with a nice sized rack. I mean you are a C, right? You should try using some makeup and doing something with your hair. That would get the guys attention. But, then again, I never said you had to have a guy. There are ways of getting laid without one."

Abigail looks at Tonya as Tonya looks her up and down smiling. Abigail awkwardly grins handing Tonya a five dollar bill. Tonya cashes her out and begins to hand the pocket change back.

"You can keep the change. Your offer is sweet, but I don't know that I am ready for the plunge into such things." Abigail rapidly brings her eyes up from Tonya's triple D breasts to her face.

"You know where to find me when the man breaks your heart," Tonya winks turning towards the back counter grabbing the towel to wipe the new mess she made.

Abigail carefully walks over to the same little wooden table she sits at every day. She takes the time to mind her foam cup to prevent any drop from spilling. She places the cup down on the table and walks around to the opposite chair sitting against the window. She adjusts her green skirt which comes down to just below her knees before she sits. She pulls the latte towards her. With her first sip, her light blue eyes scan around the coffee shop to take in the lives of the other patrons over the top edge of her cup.

Abigail notices the little old lady she has dubbed Mrs. Doubtfire. The eighty year old woman looks like Robin Williams in her blue flower dress. With all the makeup on her face, she could be a man in a latex mask. Abigail often wonders if she is really just a cross dresser, although Abigail's shy and innocent personality prevents her from asking the little old lady.

Abigail's eyes move to the business man tapping on a tablet while gulping his coffee at the next table over. Her brain kicks into gear as she notices the faded stain on his yellow tie, the scuffs on his leather deck shoes, and the small hole on his right elbow. He is a man who sits in middle management with a family. The fact he dresses nice and needs to work through his morning coffee announces to the world he is in middle management without any real power. The fact he needs to be at a coffee shop to get anything done and can't afford to replace his clothes with the slightest defect lets her know he has a wife and children. She shutters at the thought this might be what she becomes one day.

Her eyes pass over a few people she doesn't recognize in the little local shop. Abigail stops at the couple sitting in the corner booth. They are fresh out of high school with the man being only slightly older than the lady. The lady can't be older than eighteen. They are sitting so close together on the bench sipping their hot beverages. Being in the perfect position to see under the table, Abigail watches as the couple starts to play footsy.

She smiles gingerly as the man puts his hand behind his girl. As he pulls her a little closer leaning in to kiss, Abigail notices his hand slide all the way around. It slides into the arm hole of the sleeveless shirt groping her breast. Abigail looks down and away as if she had just been caught with a man groping her own breast.

Abigail gradually looks back at the couple as the longing to be fondled by a loved one fills her mind. Her eyes widen as the girl is sitting with her legs wide open leaning back ever so slightly. The man has her short skirt pulled up, holding the material back with his wrist. His finger slides the girl's underwear aside. The back of his middle finger rubs side to side against her exposed clit between her large, puffy lower lips. With her pubic hair being shaved off, the detail being seen by Abigail is arousing. The idea of such an act in public with a chance of getting caught is both scary and exciting for her. The man notices the barista Tonya look over through the reflection in the window next to them. As Tonya turns, the man nonchalantly slides his hand out from between the girl's legs and grabs his drink. The girl snaps back up into a sitting position seizing her drink from the table.

"Busted!" Abigail whispers into her cup before sipping her latte.

The man smiles as the foam cup goes to his lips. He waves with his free hand to Tonya. Tonya shakes her head giving the man her 'female's evil stink eye'. The man appears to sit up straighter, puffing out his chest as if he has earned an extra honor by being caught with his hand up someone else's skirt. Abigail giggles softly at the idea.

Chapter Two

A ding sounds behind the counter as another patron crosses the laser sensor beam at the front door. Abigail looks over to see who has decided to enjoy the wonderful atmosphere of the local shop. Her eyes widen and her mouth opens ever so slightly as she recognizes the incoming patron. With his slightly taller than average height and longer blonde hair, she recognizes Randy instantly. Abigail thinks back to her high school days and the first time she met that wonderful man.

"Class," Mrs. Thompson taps her long pointer stick on the desk repeatedly to bring attention to herself, "We have a new transfer student. His name is Randy. Randy why don't you tell us a little bit about yourself."

Randy takes a step forward without any apparent fear, "I transferred in from California. My Dad took a new job as the plant manager here."

"Please take a seat in the open desk. Class, let's begin our day." Mrs. Thompson points to a desk chair two seats in front of Abigail and one row over.

This was the first day Abigail missed out on morning announcements since she began her long enjoyable educational calling. She couldn't help but stare for the entire fifteen minutes at his soft feathery blonde hair. It was so light and fluffy. When he ran his fingers through the shoulder length hair, Abigail could see it was trimmed down to a quarter inch on the sides and back. She stared at the perfect complexion of his solid jawed face as he turned and smiled at the person on his right.

Abigail snaps out of her daydream by a deep voice

speaking to her, "Do you mind if I sit here?"

Randy is standing next to Abigail's table pointing at the chair waiting for her response, "Sure, I don't mind."

"Thanks, I thought this was going to be an uneventful summer. Glad to see someone I recognize from high school." Randy sits down taking a sip of his double chocolate latte.

"Me too," Abigail finally gets to sit and talk with Randy after all these years without being able to think of a thing to say.

Abigail looks over at the young couple. The man's hand is back up his lady's skirt. Tonya begins to walk towards the couple's stall. The man pulls his hand back above the table. The girl slouches slightly while leaning all the way back and frowns as if Tonya screwed up the moment of orgasm for her. The man takes the last gulp of his drink as Tonya gestures her thumb towards the door with a swinging arm. He gets up from the table and grabs the lady's hand. He glances over at Abigail. She quickly brings her eyes down to the table, taking a moment to glance at Randy through the corner of her eye. As her eyes fall on him, his eyes drop down to the table.

Randy glances at Abigail, whispering to her, "Wow, to be that bold. It would be exciting, but I don't think I could do it."

"I know what you mean," Abigail is confused as she had always thought he was the smooth cool kid in school who was up for anything.

The smell of wet pussy wafts over Abigail's table as the man walks past her to the door with his lady friend. The lady looks over at Abigail with a cute smirk hoping Abigail enjoyed the show. Abigail slowly turns her attention back to Randy as she realizes she did enjoy the show. He scoots his chair an inch closer as he begins to lean towards Abigail. As he leans to the left, the left side of his body straightens with his right side slouching. He barely moves any closer to her with the way his body is moving up instead of over. Abigail smiles as she realizes he is just an innocent little puppy just like her.

"I have to head off to class," Abigail looks down at the sleek silver watch on her left wrist, "It was nice seeing you again."

Randy waits until she turns towards the door to leave, "It was nice seeing you again. I don't suppose you would like to get together for lunch?"

"I would love to," Abigail turns her head back towards him with a sheepish smile, "How about Lorenzo's Little Italy Eatery at twelve thirty?"

"Sounds good to me. I will see you there." Randy quickly drops his vision down towards the edge of the table.

Abigail rushes out the door, afraid Randy will change his mind. She looks inside the coffee shop window as Randy gives an awkward wave towards her. She grins returning the wave, confident he will not disappoint. She sees Tonya walking up to Randy's table as Abigail passes the edge of the window. Abigail turns to watch where she is going as the side of her leg bumps into the bench for the barber shop next door.

Abigail barely avoids the turning barber's pole sitting just in front on the edge of the opposite side of the bench. She tucks her chin and neck down in embarrassment as the sixty year old barber turns around on the other side of the window to watch her walk by. She picks up her pace until she reaches the park with the local community college on the opposite side. She slows down taking the time to look around as she considers what having lunch with Randy may entail.

Abigail looks at the momma robin bird landing on a branch near the path to feed her chirping baby birds in the nest. The surprise smell of the lilies from the garden near the benches fills the air as another summer breeze gently passes by. She ponders why the grass seems so much greener today. The bubbling of the fountain and the little kids playing on the wooden playset in the distance presents a unique orchestra of sounds to create a melody in her head.

Abigail passes by a pair of women complaining about their husbands. One doesn't pay enough attention, while the other is too needy. Abigail doesn't hear a single word the women spew forth as examples about their men's flaws as their sounds enter the melody of the park.

"My man would never not pay attention to me," Abigail whispers to a passing squirrel several feet beyond the women's location, "And I would never get enough attention. I would take everything he has to offer, anytime he has to offer it."

As she looks at the college building approaching, she actually considers skipping school for the first time in her life. Crossing the drive to the parking lot gives her a little extra time to consider ditching. She sighs as she reaches for the long metal handle to push the two-way door open. Abigail looks at the couples in the hallways kissing and holding hands. She doesn't look away this time, even when they notice her staring. It is as if a new page has opened in her life.

"Have I finally found love?" Abigail whispers to herself in front of the classroom door.

Abigail steps into the classroom. She moves to her seat in the first row and gets ready for the lesson by placing her notebook and pen squarely on the tiny half table in front of her. Amy sits next to her and beams with an upwards curling of her mouth. Abigail smiles back examining Amy's face. The makeup is soft and gentle with just enough to make her facial features pop. Abigail turns to the front as the teacher walks in and begins the announcements three feet from the door.

Chapter Three

The announcements continue as the professor puts

his materials on the giant lab table with the projector.

Abigail isn't really paying attention today as she thinks

about Tonya suggesting Abigail should use some makeup

and do her hair for her man. Abigail's attention snaps back

to reality as the teacher finally specifies the title for

today's lecture.

"We will be discussing animal mating. It will be

important to see how several of the animals have mating

habits similar to humans. Actually, most animal mating habits can be found within the human mating habit rituals. It may only be in limited human groups as fetishes, but you will find a definite correlation to the animal kingdom somewhere within us." Mr. Goodall flips through three slides on the computer's projector as he gives the intro.

Abigail loses focus in the class as she thinks about the random chance of Tonya telling her she should get laid the same day as she runs into Randy, her high school dream boat, and the biology class talks about sex. She tunes back in as the professor describes the mating habits of the female baboon. Abigail covers her mouth with her right hand to hide the childish, embarrassed grin at the thought of running around with your butt in the air just to get some guy to shove his cock in you.

She loses focus once more and begins to think about makeup and hair styles to create animalistic color in order to attract a mate. Maybe even a little perfume to create an attractive pheromone scent. It would be a good

thing to do herself up for her luncheon. The professor calls

for a fifteen minute break as half of the class time has

passed. Abigail gets up following Amy outside to the open

air arboretum in the center of the school.

Amy lights up a cigarette as Abigail approaches her

from behind, "Hey Amy. I was wondering if you would be

willing to do me a huge favor."

"What do you need, Abigail?" Amy turns around

blowing a lung full of smoke into the air.

"Well, I have a date for lunch," Abigail fans the

smoke from another student behind her away from the

front of her face, "Could you help me do my hair and

makeup real quick?"

Amy reaches into her purse as if guided by destiny,

"I would love to give you a fifteen minute makeover!"

Abigail, moving to a nearby bench, spends the rest

of the break trying to hold her breath as Amy pulls things

out of her purse and smears them on Abigail's face. The eyes take three layers, a shadow, a liner, and something for the lashes. The face takes a strange natural color cream. The lips take two layers with lipstick applied all over and lip liner penciled on the edges. A brush and comb exit the purse last as Amy walks behind Abigail. Just as the fifteen minutes are up, Amy puts a hair tie in Abigail's hair.

"You are gorgeous! What a lucky man." Amy smashes her second cigarette butt into the ashtray next to the bench.

Abigail looks into the mirrored glass of one of the college's arboretum windows. The top part of her hair is pulled back in a braided ponytail. The bottom is left to hang. The gentle eyeliner makes her eyes pop. The lipstick is just the right color to make her lips something worth paying attention to by her Randy.

Abigail pulls on the door, holding it open, "Thank you so much. I really like how it looks."

Amy steps through the door looking back at Abigail, "He will too. We need to do this more often. I love doing hair and makeup."

The rest of the class mostly passes by in a blur. Abigail only notices where she is as the professor brings up the specifics on the sexual natures of animals and how they compare to humans. Abigail realizes she doesn't know which animal the professor is talking about most of the time, but she also doesn't really care. For the first time in her life, something has taken a more important standing over education.

Abigail thanks Amy again as class ends. She rushes out of her class and down the hall with a fervor she has never felt before. This excitement is making her nipples tingly as her breasts slightly bounce in her minimum support sports bra. She bursts through the two-way glass door and into the sunlight. She squints her eyes, turning her head to the right from the bright sunlight. Her hands twitch up a couple inches as if she is considering covering her eyes. The world outside the classroom is so bright and alive today. Her eyes quickly adjust to the intensity of the sun. She makes a beeline for the park.

Just as she is about to step off the curb of the driveway encircling the college, a blasting horn startles her. She jumps back two feet and looks at the car. The older person driving the car is screaming at her through the closed window. She buries her face part way into the textbooks she has cradled in her arms.

Abigail watches as the car passes and disappears around the corner of the school before lowering her books and looking around for other motorists. She steps off the curb. By the time she has crossed the two lane drive, she is back into her own little world and only concerned about getting to her luncheon. As she passes the fountain, she notices a red headed woman walking by. The woman's appearance shocks her back to this existence.

Three Women, Two Days, and a Night

The woman is wearing a pink low cut jersey knit top which allows most of her cleavage to show. Abigail opens her eyes slightly wider and sucks in a quick breath as she wonders if the woman is or isn't wearing a bra. It is too hard to tell on the short red head. Abigail glances back at the woman noticing her dark blue jean micro skirt just long enough to sit an inch below the woman's butt cheeks. Abigail has never really payed attention to people like this before, but for today, the vision of the woman creates new sensations of excitement deep in her loins.

Abigail turns back to her own mission, but wonders if she would ever feel confident enough to dress in such a fashion. Would a guy really prefer a woman in such skimpy apparel over a finely dressed lady? She gets to the other side of the fountain, turning to go down the path to the Italian restaurant.

She jumps slightly at a deep, yet familiar voice, "Abigail, I thought you wanted to meet at the restaurant, not the park."

"Yes," Abigail turns to find the smiling face of Randy, "What are you doing in the park?"

Randy looks down and away before coming back to Abigail's face, "I was just taking a walk since I got here a little early. Didn't realize you were going to be cutting through so soon."

"Normally I would stay and talk to my professor, but I am really looking forward to this lunch with you. So, I decided not to stick around after class let out. Granted the professor let us out ten minutes early." Abigail looks down and away after realizing she just admitted her feelings about Randy.

Randy's lips curl up and spread from ear to ear. He turns towards the restaurant putting his elbow out with his hand on his waist. Abigail hooks her arm through his appreciating his romantic gesture. They walk to the restaurant with Abigail talking about the animals and plants in the surrounding area. Randy listens to every word

as Abigail goes on and on barely stopping to take a breath.

Randy reaches towards the restaurant door as Abigail

realizes she is babbling like the depiction of a little school

girl.

Chapter Four

The door flies opens just missing Randy's hand. A

hostess holds the door welcoming them to the Italian

restaurant. Another hostess grabs two menus before

guiding them through the restaurant to their seats. Randy

walks directly behind the hostess with Abigail following

him. Abigail notices Randy tilting his head down, watching

the floor as he walks as if he is an innocent child following

his mother. The hostess seats the couple in a small corner

booth at the back of the restaurant. Randy is the polite

gentleman stepping aside with a hand gesture to let

Abigail sit first. He takes the seat opposite to her. The

hostess introduces the waiter as he walks up with pad and

pen in hand.

After their drink order, Randy looks up from his

menu, "So, what is the best meal here?"

"The chicken scampi is excellent. It is a little pricy

though." Abigail looks down at the menu a little sad at the

thought of spending so much money on a meal as she is

currently living on a small set budget.

Randy reaches out giving her menu a single tap on

the top, "I wouldn't think of skimping on a meal with you.

We shall both have the chicken scampi."

Abigail looks up with stars dancing in her eyes.

Randy grins oddly as he leans against the back of the

bench. Abigail ponders the idea of perfection as Randy

orders for them. He is gentle and a gentleman. He is

outgoing but has reservations when dealing with sex or

emotions. He is willing to go to the ends of the Earth to make her happy. Yes, Abigail believes she has found the love of her life. The meal comes to the table rather quickly as the lunch rush is in full swing. Small talk fills the air as Abigail does the majority of the chatting. Randy talks enough to keep Abigail going on about her life.

As the meal draws to the end, Randy grabs the check, "I suppose I should be going, not that I have anything to do tonight. My roommate is out of town tonight. Probably going to be a boring night."

"Maybe we should get together later," Abigail jumps at the chance to cement her relationship with Randy, "I could come over to your place. How about eight?"

Randy looks up and to the left pausing for a moment as he thinks, "It would be great to get together tonight, but my roommate's little brother is in town staying with us and I think it would be a little awkward for all of us. But, I can come over to your place if you want."

"Yes," Abigail almost pops out of her clothes as she perks up with the last words spoken to her, "Let me write down my address for you. You can be there by eight?"

"I wouldn't miss it for all the chicken scampi in the world," Randy takes the note gently brushing Abigail's fingers in the process.

Abigail watches Randy walk to the register and pay for the meal. He turns waving to her as he exits the restaurant. She lets out a heavy sigh slouching into the bench. She only sits for a moment before collecting her purse, cell phone, and book bag. She exits the restaurant heading towards the park. She needs to get to her next class. Lunch with Randy has put her behind her normal schedule. As she walks, she begins to think about skipping class again as another familiar voice brings her back to reality just past the fountain.

"Abigail, do you have a minute?" Tonya the barista

is standing near the fountain still in uniform.

Abigail turns almost bouncing in her three steps over to Tonya, "I am having the most wonderful day! Look, I took your advice about makeup and hair."

"You look beautiful, but I want to ask you something," Tonya grabs the floundering hands of her friend.

Abigail doesn't wait for the question, "I ran into Randy at the coffee shop. We met for lunch at the Italian place. It was so magical. He bought my lunch despite me ordering chicken scampi. He is so thoughtful. I am getting together with him later. It couldn't be a more perfect day."

"Abigail that is what I wanted to talk to you about. I am concerned for you. I don't mean to pry or ruin your perfect day, but Randy isn't right for you, sweetie. He is not a good man. You need to know this." Tonya cuts in trying to get Abigail back to reality.

Abigail stops bouncing pulling her hands back to

her body, "What are you talking about? You know I have liked Randy since high school. Why would you say something like that?"

"I know guys like that. I dated several of them before I knew I preferred women. They aren't good people. I don't want to see you go wrong and I don't want you to have to learn the lesson I figured out the hard way. Women were right for me." Tonya puts her hands on the upper arms of Abigail as Tonya takes a step closer.

Abigail cocks her head to the side slightly, "Right? You don't even like men. What's the big deal if I want to date one? Randy is just like me, innocent and sweet. There isn't anything bad about him."

"Remember when I went to the party our sophomore year? I got just drunk enough for Randy to take advantage of me without knowing what was going on. That was when I knew I preferred women over men. Men in general are pigs and take advantage of women, but he is a heartless bastard and far from innocent. Women don't tend to do such things to other women." Tonya removes her hands from Abigail's arms to reach for Abigail's hands again.

Abigail pulls back as she steps away from Tonya, "Just because you don't like men anymore doesn't mean he is a bad person. He isn't like that anyways. If you were that drunk maybe you just think it was him. Or, are you saying this because you're jealous of me? Do you still want him for yourself? I'm sorry, I have to get to class. I know he is right for me. We are so much alike."

"He's not anything like what you think," Tonya whispers to the wind as Abigail marches towards the college.

Abigail puts Tonya's ideas out of her head as she gets to the two-way door of the college. Abigail sits through the two afternoon classes, but thinks about what activities she will plan for tonight with Randy. She didn't think to ask what he had in mind to do tonight. She decides on asking him to pick out a movie from her collection of over two hundred DVDs. She sighs, happy to be free as the last class ends. She must get home to prepare herself for the arrival of her love and the magic of the night.

Abigail stops by the local supercenter on her way home to pick up a couple of scented candles for tonight. She walks down the grocery isle grabbing a few items for a salad. Almost bumping into a little old lady as she rounds the corner, she apologizes. Abigail grabs two manly candles with a piney outdoor scent. Randy will appreciate her thinking of him. On her way out, Abigail passes by the alcohol section. She looks at the beer and stops in the middle of the isle. Apologizing to the woman behind her for blocking the aisle, Abigail reaches for a twelve pack of domestic beer. Although she has never had any, Tonya had told her before it is a good beer.

Abigail strolls to the front to find only one cash register open. She gets in line behind the skimpy dressed woman she saw earlier in the park. Abigail stares at the woman's three inch high heel shoes. She doesn't remember if the woman had them on the last time Abigail saw her. The clothing alone was enough of a shock. The woman turns around catching Abigail who looks at the groceries in the woman's half cart.

"Like the shoes?" the woman asks looking at the beer in Abigail's cart, "I got them in Rhode Island. Got a hot date tonight? Cause I love the look."

Abigail perks up as the woman shows no signs of offense to being stared at, "Yeah, I have a special guy coming over tonight."

"Really? Lucky is what you are. I have to go over to my parents for the evening. My mom wants to cook for me whenever I am in town. I love them, but they are so boring. Plus I will probably have to listen to a lecture about how I dress like a slut." The woman drops a candy bar she

is transferring to the belt.

Abigail quickly covers her mouth as the woman

bends down to pick up the candy bar. The shirt's neckline

sags down over eight inches. The extra low opening and

the loose fit allows the shirt to expose the woman's

breasts, nipples and all. Abigail stares at the woman's

modest chest. She focuses on the large hardened nipples.

Abigail forces her eyes to quickly move to the woman's

face as Abigail realizes the woman is looking at her as she

is starting to stand. The woman smiles a sexual grin at

Abigail while swiping her card through the reader after the

clerk rings up the candy bar and announces the total for

the purchase.

The woman glances back as Abigail empties her

cart, "Have a good night and good luck with your date. It

was nice to meet you."

Abigail turns giving a little nod and a wave. She

steers clear of making eye contact with anyone else in the store as if they would have any idea she was staring at another woman's breasts. Abigail gets back to her apartment as quickly as she can keeping her eyes on the ground. She juggles everything in her hands as she tries to unlock her door in a hurry. The door only opens half way before Abigail squeezes through the gap, slamming it shut behind her. She leans against the door as if she is only now safe from the people knowing she had looked at another woman sexually. She lets out a heavy sigh of relief.

Chapter Five

Abigail puts her groceries away in the kitchen. She only has three hours before Randy will be at her door to watch a movie. She walks around the one bedroom apartment looking for anything out of place. The damp hand washed bra hanging in the bathroom on the towel bar near the monthly pads which are poised on the counter are both placed in the cupboard under the bathroom sink. The little frilly pillows all smooshed on one side of the small couch where she fell asleep last night are spread out to make it look inviting. The underwear hanging on the bed post, where she threw them this morning trying to get out the door for coffee, are tossed in the closet to hide them. She stops in the living room scanning the apartment. She places the two candles on the little sofa table behind her couch. She lights them to allow time for the odor to accumulate. All is good in the world of Abigail.

Forty five minutes has passed as she spent the time to note every detail of the cleanliness of her apartment. Abigail walks into her bedroom. She drops her skirt to the floor. She uses her right foot to fling it into the air, awkwardly catching it. After tossing it in the closet with the bedpost underwear, she pulls out a pair of jeans. Sliding them on, she moves to the living room to check her apparel in front of the full sized mirror. Abigail is happy with her decision in clothing for her date knowing Randy will find her appearance appealing.

Abigail decides it is time to eat dinner. She goes to the kitchen pulling out the salad fixings and lettuce. As she chops, she realizes she has not planned anything for snacks while they watch a movie. She sets the salad aside for a moment to scrounge through her cupboards.

"Ah-ha!" Abigail exclaims as she finds two bags of microwave popcorn.

Abigail sets them on the counter, also pulling out a bowl to fill later when she nukes the popcorn. She returns to her salad. As she finishes putting a light coating of Thousand Island dressing on the salad, she looks at the clock. She only has an hour and a half until Randy arrives. Abigail moans as she flails her arms and jerks her body. Time will just not move fast enough for her. She moves to the little two chair table just off her kitchen.

She eats her salad slowly losing herself in a book she has spent the last week reading in her free time. Half way through her salad she decides to put on some music.

Scouring through her cd collection, she has trouble deciding which disc to play. She finally decides on a slow instrumental symphony who had played in Australia. She sits down returning to her book. As she takes the last bite of salad, she looks up at the clock.

She chokes down her last bite. Randy is going to be here in ten minutes. She quickly closes the book, scoops up her dishes, and rises them in the sink. She turns to walk to the bathroom to brush her teeth just as the apartment reverberates a pounding on the door. Abigail's eyes widen as she freezes in place. Randy is early.

Abigail moves to the door wiping her hand on her pants. She can feel the excess sweat just dripping off as her heart beats in her throat. She reaches for the doorknob slowly. Her heart is beating even harder. She can hear her labored breathing over the sound of her heart.

Abigail opens the door to find Randy standing with a single rose outstretched, "This is for you."

Three Women, Two Days, and a Night

"Thank you, it's beautiful," Abigail takes the extended rose, pushing it up to her nose.

Randy rubs the palm of his hand on his pants at the pocket, "Not as pretty as you though."

He reaches out towards Abigail, "You have sauce on your chin."

Randy places his thumb on her chin to wipe off the sauce. The tip of his thumb lightly brushes across her bottom lip from one side to the other. Abigail softly twitches as a chill runs up her spine. She steps back gesturing for Randy to come in. Abigail peers out the crack in the door as she slowly shuts it to look for anyone who might be watching in the hallway. Satisfied there is no reason to be embarrassed, Abigail embraces the moment as she turns around.

"I thought we might watch a movie tonight. There is a bookshelf with all of my DVDs by the bathroom." Abigail points to the door sitting slightly open, "We can watch any one you want."

Randy saunters over with his hands bashfully in his pockets, "Well, which one do you think is the most romantic movie?"

"Easy. Casablanca is my all-time favorite romantic movie. Have you seen it?" Abigail puts a bag of popcorn into the microwave.

Randy looks over the DVDs finding Casablanca rather quickly as it sits near the top of the collection, "No, did you want to introduce it to me?"

"I would love to. I will have the popcorn ready in just a few minutes." Abigail impatiently fidgets in the kitchen waiting for the microwave to go off.

With the popcorn done, Abigail walks into the living room and sits on the love seat she claims as a small couch. It was the biggest couch she could find which would fit into her apartment. Randy drops the DVD into the machine. He looks at the love seat and pauses. The tip of his foot begins to sway as it lifts off the floor. He returns

his hands to his pockets as his eyes move from the floor to

the empty seat so very close to Abigail. Abigail smiles

patting the seat next to her.

Randy sits down as Abigail starts the movie. Abigail

swings her feet up under her on the side opposite to

Randy. This brings her body in close to his. His right arm

gets in the way of them sitting comfortably, so he moves it

to the back of the couch a little bit awkwardly. Abigail oohs

as the intro scene appears on the television. She rests her

head against Randy's shoulder. She has never felt so

comfortable with anyone before. It seems as if fate is

working in her favor finding her soulmate. The movie

progresses scene after scene as the couple enjoys the

popcorn. Abigail sits contently with her head on Randy's

shoulder.

About twenty minutes into the movie, Randy's arm

slides off the back of the couch landing on Abigail, "I'm so sorry. I didn't mean to let it fall and ruin the moment."

"I don't mind. Maybe you should just leave it there so it doesn't fall again." Abigail reaches around with her other arm and pats his hand.

Randy smiles as the movie continues to play. After another twelve minutes, a scene change comes giving a mild surprise. Randy jumps slightly. His hand flies up Abigail's side accidently cupping her breast. Randy pulls his hand away quickly and shifts his body, embarrassed at the fact he groped a breast.

"I'm sorry, the scene change startled me," Randy looks down as Abigail looks towards her breast.

Abigail takes his hand pulling it over her shoulder to rest in the air in front of her, "You can relax. It isn't a big deal. It is easy to get caught up in this movie. That is one of the reasons I love it so much."

Randy's hand and arm relax. The tip of his hand rests just under Abigail's breast with his palm and fingers sitting out a half inch from grabbing position. His thumb

supports his hand as it sits on the outside of her clothing,

yet expertly positioned for her nipple.

Randy shifts the weight of his hand to his upper

arm as it rests on her shoulder. He slowly moves his thumb

back and forth across her nipple with just enough pressure

to be felt but not enough to be highly noticeable. Abigail

breathes in deeply after a few minutes. Her nipple is

starting to get hard and has a strange tingle. Abigail lets

out an mm-uh with a shivering of her body. She realizes

her pussy is wet enough to make her underwear damp.

Randy starts to pull his hand back as she looks down.

Abigail grabs his arm, forcing the hand back into position.

Randy applies a little more pressure to his thumb and

switches to a counter clockwise rotation.

Chapter Six

Abigail finds herself breathing deeply. She has

never felt such an intense sensation like this before from

her nipple. After three more minutes of gratification and

only thinking of greater intensity, she reaches down

grabbing the bottom of her shirt. She lifts the shirt up over

her bra to remove the obstruction. Randy rubs on the

outside of the bra for a brief moment. He slides his hand

up, slipping it between her bra and breast. His hand slides

down to the hardened nipple, rubbing up and down. After

only a second or two, Randy traps Abigail's nipple between

her bra and his fingers.

"Ow," Abigail somewhat jerks her body back away

from Randy's hand stretching the bra.

Randy looks down at Abigail as she looks up,

"Sorry, this is difficult with a bra on. Do you want me to

just rub on the outside of the bra?"

"No, it should just come off," Abigail quickly gets

back into the mood as the innocence pours from Randy's

mistake and obvious inexperience with women.

Randy reaches in back of Abigail as she leans

forward slightly, holding the back of her shirt up above the

bra strap. With two fingers Randy clasps the bra's hooks.

He pinches them together a tad. Then his thumb applies

pressure towards Abigail's back while his finger pulls away

from her back and towards the base of the thumb. The bra

comes unhooked in record time.

Randy places his right hand on Abigail's back giving

two medium pressured rubs up and down before sliding

his hand along her side popping both breasts out of the

bra and letting her lean back again. He palms her right

breast giving a firm squeeze as she turns her head for a

kiss. He allows the breast to slide out of his hand slowly as

he squeezes until only the nipple remains between his

thumb and pointer finger, also ending the kiss. He applies

light pressure rotating the nipple back and forth.

Abigail lets out a moan. Randy returns to the

counter clockwise rotation as his body slides down on the

couch. The slide down is just enough to place Abigail's left

hand resting on the jeans directly over his cock. He

extends his left arm around her neck and over her

shoulder to rub the other nipple.

Abigail tilts her head back applying pressure with

her hand to Randy's cock. Her moaning increases as the

pleasure from her breasts overwhelms her senses. She

begins to rub up and down on Randy's jeans as his sexual

muscle begins to harden and throb. Randy pulsates his rear muscles in a small gentle tightening and release motion. His cock raises up and down only a half inch pushing against Abigail's hand. Abigail doesn't understand why, but between the feelings of excitement in her breasts, the moisture draining from her pussy, and the pulsating of Randy's cock, she unzips his jeans to let the monkey out of his pants as it silently screams to her to be set free.

Abigail stops undoing the jeans as she quickly sucks in air leaning her head back. It is the first time she has ever climaxed in any sexual manner, although it has been building all day. She didn't even know playing with your breasts could give an orgasm, even if just a little one. Her small orgasm is enough to finish soaking her panties. Randy slides his right hand off her breast, down her stomach, and gracefully under her pants and panties. He applies pressure to her hairy pubic region slowly pulling back up towards her breast. Abigail arches her back as her second tiny orgasm comes. Randy slides his left hand up over her shoulder and drops it down to his pants. In half a flash, Randy undoes the jeans the rest of the way opening the front. He slides his underwear down in the front to allow his throbbing organ to escape and find Abigail's bare hand.

Abigail wraps her hand around his prick, clutching as Randy's right hand releases pressure from her breast, slides down a little closer to her clit, and applies pressure in an upward motion again with the skill to not pull on the pubic hair. She sucks in a deep breath holding it for a moment before releasing. She realizes what she is holding, and although momentarily confused about how it got there, she starts to stroke up and down still applying pressure. His mmm raises her excitement level as she is giving to him, for her first time, what she is getting from him.

Abigail whispers so the mood will not go fleeting out the door, "Let's move to the bedroom so we have more space."

"I think you're right," Randy slides his right hand off of her breast along her side around to her upper back.

Abigail gets up for a moment then pauses to remove her shirt. She reaches back grabbing Randy's hand to lead him to the bedroom in a romantic gesture. As Randy gets up from the couch, he uses his free left hand to dislodge his underwear. His pants and underwear fall to the floor. He steps out of them as Abigail pulls on his hand towards the bedroom. A slight tug backwards on her arm shifts her upper body causing her C cups to bounce. She looks at the full size body mirror on the wall. She watches Randy smile as her tits bounce.

"Like that? Then how about this?" Abigail turns towards Randy and jumps four inches into the air.

Abigail's C cups fly into the air as her body comes

down. The breasts bounce up and down several times as if an earthquake is sending aftershocks. Randy grins ear to ear as he watches them until they stop bouncing. Abigail spins around pulling him into the bedroom with Randy keeping both eyes on the mirror to watch her breasts sway back and forth until out of sight.

Randy stops her just before the bed. The palms of his hands land on her hips. He is still holding tight to her right hand with their fingers interlaced. His left hand glides around until it reaches the button of her jeans. A quick flip of the fingers unbuttons the pants. He slips his fingers down grabbing the zipper to go along for the ride. Abigail slides her feet to shoulder width apart. Her jeans fall to the ground with only a slight nudge from Randy.

Randy guides the hand interlaced with hers around her pelvis and down between the low riding underwear and bare flesh. Abigail pushes her body back against him as her hand becomes wet from her pussy. The combination of Randy and herself rubbing against her clit stimulates her in a new way. Randy rubs up and down a couple times before leaving her hand to play with her clit. He bends at the knees lowering himself to head level with her small shapely backside. He grips the underwear on both sides sliding the panties down her legs. He shifts his head forward opening his mouth. He grabs the bottom curve of her right cheek with his lips, sucking in giving a big kiss.

Randy touches her ankles with the tips of his fingers. Abigail continues to gently rub her clit. His fingers run up her legs while he switches to an upright position. His hands slide forward around to her belly as they pass over her hips. He presses his body to hers as his hands glide upward, grasping her breasts in his hands and giving a firm squeeze. He pushes with his pelvis hard enough to slip his cock between her cheeks. She takes a deep breath with another new experience as she realizes what she is feeling against her anus. She removes her hand from between her legs, bending one leg to let the knee rest on the bed. Her arms extend forward to catch her as her upper body leans forward. The repositioning slides his love muscle to rest on her clit. She closes her eyes, slowly breathing in as his throbbing pulsations are pressing hard against her clit.

Chapter Seven

Abigail crawls forward on the bed flipping over so

her head lands on the pillow. Randy stares at her naked

body and bouncing breasts until her eyes land on his. He

reaches across his body with his arms wrenching the shirt

up and off. He gives a bound, landing on the bed next to

her on the right side. Her tits bounce back and forth from

her face to her tight stomach while leaning over towards

her sides. Randy puts his left hand on the side of her head.

His palm sits just below her ear with his thumb going up

her face in front of the ear. His fingers are spread on the back of her head and neck. He leans over her, his hard cock pressing into her hip, kissing her deeply and passionately.

As he pulls his head back, his left hand glides down from her head along her body to the bushy pubic hair. His right arm slides under her head and pillow gripping onto her right shoulder. He lifts himself onto his side with his right elbow, slipping his left hand between her legs to her inner thigh. A gentle pull of the hands gestures for Abigail to roll onto her right side. Randy lowers himself behind her. His throbbing meat pushes between her cheeks as his left hand guides her leg to bend up and over his. His right hand slithers out from beneath her, engulfing her left breast.

Randy shifts his pelvis back. His cock slides down between Abigail's cheeks. Her right hand grabs the edge of the pillow with expectation. Her left hand crumples the comforter they are laying on twelve inches out from her stomach. She sucks air in twice in quick secession as the head pushes against her tight little anus. It slides by, popping out under her as Randy moves quickly at the end. The head comes to rest on her swollen clit as it bounces back towards her. She shivers with the impact. Randy shifts his pelvis again to slide the head to the flowing wet hole of her expecting pussy.

Randy's left hand slides up her leg while the tip of his cock slips in and out of the hole making Abigail suck in air with every entry. Randy's left hand moves to her right breast. Both hands grip the areola of the tit they surround, grasping tight. Randy pinches the nipples as he pulls them out an inch. His cock slides into the wet hole breaking the firmness of Abigail's virginity.

With Randy covering the pain of losing her virginity by pinching her nipples, Abigail lurches her back causing Randy to pull the nipples out almost two additional inches and towards the center of her chest. His cock reaches full depth as Abigail lets out a passionate scream. Randy pulls his cock back an inch and pushes back to full depth while releasing the pull on the nipples without fully losing his grip. Abigail releases her back muscles as the orgasm ends. She can feel the wetness flow out of her, over Randy's penis, and down the back of her right leg. She pushes her ass into his pelvis to get as much of him inside her as possible. She grunts loudly as she finally knows the pleasures of a man.

As soon as she grunts, Randy begins to move in and out in a slow rhythmic fashion. He uncrosses his arms switching the grip upon her breasts, now with matching hand to breast. With his arms extending as he switches breasts, he leans back giving him a better position to increase his speed. Every other thrust of his hard cock increases in speed. Both Abigail and Randy let out grunts and moans in the entanglement of making love.

Three Women, Two Days, and a Night

Within a few minutes, Randy drops his hands from her breasts. His hands quickly fly through the air to grab onto her skinny hips. His upper body is partially mimicking the motion of his lower as he not only is thrusting fast, but as hard as he can muster.

"Ow," Abigail breaks out of the ecstasy of the moment, "You're starting to hurt me. You need to not go so fast and hard."

Ugh is the only response from Randy with no change to his movements. Abigail starts to shift in order to reach back to get his attention. Randy's hands are strong, holding her hips in place, preventing her from shifting. Abigail begins to cry out to Randy as he groans followed by an ugh. He slides his arms in grabbing her breasts harder and firmer than before. The tremors of his body brings Abigail to an unknown happy place despite the pain. She closes her eyes, puts her hands over his, and rides the emotion of the pleasure she is sure Randy is feeling right now. She passes the feeling of pain and wraps herself back into the romance of losing her virginity to her love. As Randy's tremors and groaning ends, the feeling of him expanding and contracting inside her as he lets his cum flow fills her with the ecstasy she expected, removing the memory of any pain she felt. Abigail shifts her shoulders back and forth to scoot in closer to his chest.

Randy sits holding her for the briefest of moments. He releases the iron grip on her tits. A heavy, sad sigh comes from Abigail as he slides his arms out from underneath her and quickly pulls his cock from inside her. She turns to look over at him while still laying on her side. She watches as he flops over onto his back. She feels the mix of their cum draining out of her crotch and onto her leg.

"That was great. Glad we bumped into each other at the coffee shop." Randy lifts his right hand letting it land on her left ass cheek with a light slapping noise.

Abigail rolls onto her belly watching Randy's face, "You hurt me near the end."

"I'm sorry," Randy looks over with a big eyed puppy dog look, "I guess I just got overly excited. You really can't blame me. Have you looked at yourself in the mirror lately?"

Abigail feels the mix of their cum continue to gush from her. Never having felt it before, she squirms slightly due to the strange tickling sensation. Randy smiles before sitting up. His right hand comes up and down again giving her another light tap, this time on her right cheek. His hand hits the bed putting pressure down to lift himself slightly. He does a bumping scoot until he reaches the end of the bed. Randy heads right for the bathroom.

Abigail lays there in the moment of bliss as she listens to Randy pee and then wash up. Washing takes longer than she expected, as if he is washing more than just his hands. She patiently waits for him on the bed knowing he will return to her. Randy walks into the bedroom and stands at the foot of the bed. She rolls over onto her back with a scrunched face as he doesn't come back to bed.

Abigail watches as his penis rapidly shrinks to an unhardened state, "Are you going to come back to bed?"

Randy looks at her briefly before scanning the room for his lost t-shirt, "No, I would love to. But, I need to get back before my roommate's brother burns down the joint. Besides my roommate will be returning soon and I don't want to be caught abandoning the little brother."

"I understand," Abigail sighs as the perfect moment fades just a little, "I suppose we can do coffee in the morning. Will that work?"

Randy heads into the living room to retrieve his pants and underwear as his voice echoes into the room, "I will have to call you to let you know. I am leaving town tomorrow and returning to college. I will check my schedule and get back to you."

Randy pops his head into the room. He walks to the bed. Leaning over, he kisses her right nipple with a loud smacking noise. He gives a flirting good-bye and Abigail halfheartedly returns the farewell. She hears the front door open and close.

Abigail turns to the window, "I know you had to go. It is good I found a responsible man. Tonya was right about needing to get laid. I have to say I feel really relaxed right now."

Abigail lays in bed for another ten minutes enjoying the feeling of bliss created by the hormones she produced during her session of love making with Randy. As she finally starts to get up, she feels squishy between her legs and butt cheeks. She spreads her legs leaning to her right. Looking down, she sees cum all over between her legs and a giant wet spot on the comforter. She groans as she rolls the rest of the way off the side of the bed. She glances at the bedroom door.

Abigail feels a sense of relief about Randy leaving. She notices a pinkish coloring to part of the cum staining the bed. It is the final untidy sign of the virginity given to her love. Such a mess would be embarrassing. She grabs her comforter at the top zipping it off the bottom of the bed with a single snap of her arm. She throws it into a laundry basket sitting just inside the living room as she passes to the bathroom. She turns the switches on for the light and the fan. She giggles at the sight of the toilet seat being left up. She drops the seat down as she turns to the faucet in the shower.

Chapter Eight

Getting the water just right, Abigail pulls the

curtain closed on the faucet end, moving to the opposite

side of the tub. She steps in carefully, using her leg to

double check the water temperature once more before

getting inside the tub. She turns backwards leaning her

head into the stream of warm water. She sits for a

moment letting the water slide down her naked body as

the sensation of the night stays alive in her mind and

heart.

Abigail reaches up for the bottle of shampoo. She sticks one hand under the pump using the other to squirt the fluid out into her hand. She giggles and squirts a second shot into her hand as she imagines it is the hard cock of Randy squirting just for her. She rubs the shampoo in for a couple minutes. She takes her time rinsing as her mind wanders back into the bedroom. Her mind returns to reality with a curling of the corners of her lips upwards and a sigh. She steps out from under the flow of water.

She grabs her scrubby putting on the usual dose of body wash. She stops for a moment looking down at her cum soaked legs and hairy crotch. She moves the scrubby back under the body wash bottle giving an extra squirt. She applies the scrubby to her stomach in a circular fashion so the extra soap will transfer down after washing her upper body. She moves the scrubby up to her right breast. She winces pulling the scrubby away from her body while moving her body back away from the scrubby.

Three Women, Two Days, and a Night

Abigail is just realizing how sore her breast is after enjoying the slightly brutal iron grip of Randy. She uses her hands to gently caress the soap onto her sore breasts and extremely tender nipples. She reapplies the scrubby to wash her arms and delicately shaved pits.

Abigail starts to hum the only love song she knows by heart. Her scrubby leaves a trail of bubbles from her armpit down her side ensuring to avoid her breasts. She slips through her soapy stomach moving to scrubby her other side. The scrubby circles her stomach to pick up extra soap as she breaks out into full verse. She moves the scrubby down her left leg and back up her right going all the way around the legs. Her left leg hoists up into the air as she hits the main stanza of the song. It lands on the edge of the tub leaving her in the perfect position to finish her cleanup.

The coolness of being out from under the water with legs spread, and with the special activities performed in the early night hours, Abigail relaxes her stomach as she begins to let flow a golden stream into the tub. She quickly uses one hand to move the curtain back far enough for her to see out the bathroom door. The entire time she creates a golden shower in the tub, she watches to ensure Randy does not come back. It will be devastatingly humiliating if Randy catches her peeing in the shower.

As Abigail finishes, she releases the shower curtain. She makes sure it goes back into the original position. She relaxes, letting out one last little squirt. She giggles this time as there is no chance of being caught. Returning to her love song, she pivots the scrubby to the inside of her left leg. She pauses for a moment just before the scrubby touches her crotch.

"No sense making the same mistake twice," Abigail puts the words to the tune of the love song.

She soaps up her right hand gently applying it to her pussy lips. Her eyes open wide as her chin dropping stretches her face. The lack of pain catches her off guard.

She closes her eyes as the fingers glide over her clit. The

excitement of the night still in her mind, her simple

cleaning causes the delight to resurface. She stands for a

moment rubbing back and forth with her eyes closed. She

shifts her weight causing her right foot to slide three

inches in the tub. Her eyes jerk open. The exhilaration

goes down the drain.

She begins to sing the song again from the

beginning. Stepping under the water, the soap flows from

her body. Abigail spins cautiously, continuing the song as

the water gurgles entering her mouth. She bends down

spitting the water out laughing. Her hand flies across the

top of the twin knobs controlling the water. The hot turns

off, but the cold sticks a little. Abigail screams murder as

the ice cold water hits her breasts hardening her nipples.

The pain is intense causing her to ignore the ice cold water

on the rest of her body.

Abigail grabs the cold knob with a firm grip giving it a hard twist. The cold water drips three drops from the shower head. Abigail shivers as the shower curtain is removed. She grabs an oversized fluffy pink bath towel. She presses it against the hardened nipples trying to warm them. She dries quickly as her skinny body holds little water. She wraps her hair in a second towel sitting on the counter giving a little twist at the end.

Without thinking about the possible embarrassment, Abigail does a first by walking out of the bathroom without having her body clothed or wrapped. She dances her way into the kitchen stopping to wiggle her tiny butt up and down as she bends over in the middle of the living room. She flips the cupboard open spinning around before grabbing a plastic cup. The fridge opens with her bending inside to grab the apple juice. The knees bending bounce her up and down with her tits swinging back and forth into the cold of the fridge. This quickly reminds her of the tenderness of her breasts slowing her

dance until the fridge door shuts.

She pours a glass of juice, quickly opening and

closing the fridge door to place the carton back onto its

shelf. She takes a big gulp of juice before side thrusting her

hips in an attempt to dance back into the living room. She

finishes her drink placing the empty cup on the coffee

table. She swings herself back into the bedroom. Her left

hand grabs the towel on her head flinging it onto a small

chair in the corner of the room. She spins around throwing

her arms out and falling backwards onto the bed. She lets

out a heavy sigh before flipping over. Her crawl to the

pillow takes her back to the beginning of the night. She

flops down face first into the pillow, happy and content as

her life could not get any more perfect.

She turns on her left side. Her right knee bends

bringing her foot up and creating a gap between her legs.

She sniffs at the pillow Randy had laid upon. Her hand

pushes its way down between her legs. She stops as soon

as her fingers provide pressure onto her crotch. Her

shoulder jerks. She slowly removes her hand. The levels of

ecstasy and endorphins have faded significantly. The look

of shock on her face says it all, the pain of the pounding

her pussy took has now taken its toll. Even so, the face

returns to a smile as the thought of what would be

tomorrow reenters her mind. She lowers her leg, closes

her eyes, and falls asleep naked on top of the sheets.

Another act in a long line of firsts for the little book worm.

Abigail awakens abruptly. She looks at her alarm

clock glowing green on her night stand. The chill of the

night has set in. She touches her breasts with her right

hand quickly removing the hand to hover a few inches

away. The hand gently moves back into place. Her left

hand slides along the sheet to comfort the throbbing pain

coming from between her legs. She sobs slightly. The

thought of physical pain without the man she gave her

virginity to in order to comfort her never entered her mind. Actually, she did not realize the amount of pain she would be in after such an act. She sobs for a moment whispering Randy's name.

Alone and cold, Abigail gets off the bed grabbing the soiled comforter from the laundry basket. She throws it on the bed. Crawling under the sheets is a little chilly, but not as bad as the early morning air. She lays her head on the pillow, eyes wide open. The digital number of the minutes changes several times before her eyes close. The troubled sleep is interrupted by a loud beeping noise.

Chapter Nine

A brunette haired woman walks out of the coffee shop, stopping on the edge of the sidewalk. She takes a sip of her mochaccino and squints upwards at the sun bouncing off the few surrounding sky scrapers a block away from the shop. She takes one step closer to the curb just as a red headed woman coming from across the street tries to slip past her to avoid a bike messenger whipping by with little regard to the pedestrians and motorists.

"Ow," The brunette haired woman switches the

hand holding the mochaccino as hot liquid spills on her thumb and down the back of her now free hand.

"Sorry, the bike messenger came faster than I thought he would," The redhead watches as the brunette haired woman shakes the hot liquid from her burning hand.

The brunette haired woman curls one side of her mouth in a sexual mannerism, "It's not a big deal. Happens from time to time on my own. Even this can't ruin today."

The brunette haired woman looks up at the pedestrian crossing symbol as the redhead steps past her. Despite the sign being a little person walking in white, she looks both ways before stepping into the street. Half way across the street, she looks down at her bag as the cell phone inside makes a woot-woo sound. She waits until she gets to the other curb to pause, digging the phone out of her large stylish brown leather purse.

The woman hits the little button on the side of the

phone and flips her thumb across the screen. Her thumb taps the little yellow envelope for messaging. The list of contacts comes up with a little orange circle and a one next to John. She touches the screen to open the text.

"Jill, see you at work. You need to open. Stopping by store to get more printer paper and discs. Be ten minutes late." The message from John is short, sweet, and choppy.

Jill taps the dialog box and one-thumbs the message back, "Okay boss. Will see you there. We are still good to meet tonight, yes?"

"We are. Will see you at work, sweet cheeks." John's message seems preplanned as fast as it comes back.

Jill holds the home button and clears all the programs sitting in queue. She taps the button to turn the screen off. She slips the phone back into her purse. Walking down half the block, she turns towards a maroon minivan. She passes around the front peering out before she heads to the driver's door. Her hand finds the keys inside the immense clutter of the purse. Her thumb hits the unlock button before the keys see the summer sun.

The drive to the office takes little time as the roads are surprisingly unbound by traffic. Jill collects her purse before exiting the minivan. She reaches back grabbing the side door handle with her left hand as her rump leaves the seat. Little effort is needed to pop the side door open as she is a stocky woman. She grabs an extra-large tote from the back seat. As the side door slams shut, Jill pauses to look at her image in the door window and panel. The door distorts her image making her look fatter than the normal pudginess she sees in the mirror every day.

With a heavy sigh, Jill turns to the front office door. She unlocks the glass door. The arm with the purse bends at the elbow reaching up to the lettering to clear a finger print below the 'I' with the cuff of her sleeve. She looks at the lettering stating 'Wilcock Investments and Portfolios'.

The door glides open. Jill hits the switch next to the door with her purse elbow causing all of the lights to turn on. The open sign blinks a couple of times before glowing a steady neon red.

Jill looks at the different memos and pictures of the stock world posted on the wall in the entry way as she passes them. She walks around the little dividing wall separating the entry from the main office area. The archway in the dividing wall opens into a fifteen by fifteen foot room with two desks, more pictures, more memos, a full body mirror, and a single door in the middle across the room from the arch.

Jill sets the tote on a chair next to the mirror. She turns to look at the sign just above the mirror. 'This will begin your future'. She drops her gaze down to the mirror. She turns back and forth rotating the image to look at her sides from different angles. She pushes gently on her face. The skin moves erasing the wrinkles around her eyes.

Releasing the skin allows the wrinkles to magically reappear. She bats her eyes a couple times looking at the unusual makeup over her eyes.

Bringing her vision down, Jill looks at her shirt. She tugs at the skin tight business shirt. The extra weight she carries around her mid-section depresses her. It is no wonder her husband has made insufficient advances towards her sexually as of late. Her focus goes to the buttons on the shirt. With the shirt already having the top two buttons undone, she slowly brings her hand up undoing one more. She tugs the sides of her shirt down to make sure it sits properly on her.

Jill focuses on her breasts. With three buttons undone, the rim of her brand new silky push-up demi bra just shows through. The new bra is a cup small to force a large amount of spillage out the top, especially with the extreme push-up. She examines the rim of the bra since it is now visible. A little touch of her areola can be seen outside the bra. Her mind ponders an idea. She quickly rocks onto her toes giving a one inch bounce off the ground. As she lands, the left nipple slips out from the bra becoming visible in the mirror.

Jill laughs, tilts her head to the side, and wonders if leaving it out would help get her husband excited. Her vision goes back to the full picture in the mirror. She lets out a heavy sigh as the forty year old fat body in the mirror disturbs her. She pulls on the bra with her left hand and uses her right hand to tuck her nipple back under. Releasing the bra, the breast is still not sitting properly. She begins to readjust a second time as a chime goes unnoticed.

The third time she readjusts, she hears a gravelly voice behind her, "Would you like a hand with that? Or, you could just go without. That would fix the problem."

Jill looks up at the mirror to see her fifty year old boss looking over her shoulder at her hands down her bra,

"No, boss. I got it this time. Maybe next time you can help and it will take less time to get it right."

"I got all the supplies from the store. I will bring them in after my meeting with Henry Tustin. He should be here in the next twenty minutes." The boss curls the edges of his mouth as it opens to let out a deep toned laugh.

The boss walks into the separated office to set up for the day before his appointment arrives. Jill grabs the tote, dropping it by her desk on the floor. She pulls the high back executive chair backwards enough to gain access to the desk. Her purse is gently swung under the desk where the chair usually goes. She lowers herself down halfway into the chair before she plops down. She stands halfway back up to fix her tight fitting mid-thigh mini skirt. She lowers herself back down so the skirt won't ride up.

Chapter Ten

Jill looks down at her breast as her nipple feels a slight chill. Both nipples have popped out of the bra this time. She struggles to get both breasts back in and sitting comfortably. With five minutes invested since she got to work in adjusting her bra, she is settled into her chair to start her day.

The boss walks out of the office reading a paper, "Jill, have you seen the stock analysis report Tonya printed out yesterday?"

Three Women, Two Days, and a Night

"Here it is," Jill pulls the report off the top of a stack of papers holding it up for him, "Problem?"

"From my viewpoint, the only problem I have won't be addressed until tonight," The boss steps next to her chair taking the paper while looking down Jill's blouse.

Jill turns her chair to face the boss with her vision right at his waist, "Is it really that big of a tease, John?"

"You have no idea. It will be a distraction all day. Major problem." John sticks out his pointer finger and runs it from the side of Jill's face, down her neck, and to the bra line on her breast.

Jill slowly reaches up grabbing the button on his pants and popping it open as if she is not sure about her actions. John's eyes widen as this behavior seems to catch him off guard. Jill pulls on both side flaps of the khaki's opening causing the zipper to fly down to the bottom. She pulls down the front of his pants. His half hard penis flops out into the office light. Her right hand slides over the puffy cone shaped head of his penis, curling around the semi-soft flesh of the stalk. Pulling her hand away from John, the skin partially folds over itself. Pushing back towards him, the skin tightens along the shaft. She leans forward sticking her tongue out as far as it will go. The tongue goes under the head, reaching back while sitting millimeters below his cock until the tip of the penis head touches her lips. Jill brings her tongue up to press against the underside all at once. She pulls the tongue back, sliding it into her mouth while keeping the tip of his head resting on her upper lip.

Jill looks up while moving her hand forward and back, feeling the half hard penis turn into a rock hard cock, "Now that might be a problem. Too much of a tease?"

"Only if you stop now," John stares deep into Jill's eyes, "Why don't you stick it in before we get interrupted?"

Jill's eyes drop back down to the stone pillar in her

hand. Her hand keeps jerking forwards and back, although it is starting to get tiresome for her. She leans her head forward sticking the puffy cone head into her mouth. John moans instantly. She continues to jerk the bottom half while bobbing her head to suck on the top half. Her tongue rotates between rubbing the bottom of the head to flicking just behind the head. John's leans back with his upper body, his eyes close, and his right hand rests itself on the back of Jill's head. His hand opens and closes with the rhythm of her head thrusts.

Just as John begins to moan a little louder, and a little more frequently, a bump on the front door distracts them both. Jill releases the cock from the curved grip of her hand and pulls her head back with a loud smacking noise from the suction as the lips come off the tip. John steps back fixing his pants and shirt as the door swings open. The ding of someone entering sounds through the office. Jill swings her chair around to face the door. John darts into his office to finish correcting himself before the meeting with the client.

Jill fixes her gaze on the guest as he rounds the wall, "Welcome Mr. Tustin, Mr. Cardiff will be right with you."

"Well, thank you little lady. Have I had the pleasure?" Mr. Tustin stares at the provocatively dressed secretary.

"No sir, we have not," Jill looks at the eighteen inch stack of paperwork next to her twenty three inch monitor, "I only work two days a week."

The office door opens with John stepping out, "Mr. Tustin, glad to see you. Will you please step into my office?"

"You really have some nice eye candy around here. Shame Tonya isn't here. Add in that young one and it would be a candy shop today." Mr. Tustin can be overheard by Jill as John closes the door.

Jill thinks about Tonya, John's other secretary. She works part-time as well. Three days a week here. She wonders, with the plump body and bigger breasts, if the boss is also playing around with her. Shaking the thoughts from her head, Jill reaches for the papers on the top of her stack. She sits verifying the information on the forms and entering the data into the computer. On occasion, she hits the print button on her keyboard. The printer across the room behind Tonya's desk comes alive. Jill glances at the printer every time it stops to ensure the printer didn't halt due to a malfunction.

Jill gets up from her desk as the inner office door opens. John gestures the client into the main office area. Mr. Tustin makes his goodbyes and heads across the room to the archway. He takes a single glance back to ogle over Jill.

John waits until Mr. Tustin is out of the office before handing the paperwork to Jill, "I don't suppose you would like to finish what we started?"

"Do you have time?" Jill asks walking over to the filing cabinet next to Tonya's desk.

John walks over reaching around Jill and grabbing firm to her breasts, "For you, I would always make the time."

John pulls with his right arm and pushes with his left while turning his hips to the right. Jill takes small steps sideways to turn with him. He pushes his upper body against hers just enough to get her to bend over Tonya's wood top desk. Jill reaches behind her pulling the skirt up and over till it bunches up on her waist. John undoes and drops the front of his pants and underwear. Jill reaches back again pulling the bikini underwear down to her knees. The underwear falls the rest of the way to her ankles.

John reaches forward placing his hand against her right butt cheek, "Now that is a fine thing to behold."

John rubs up and down rotating between both

cheeks with his hand for almost a full minute. Jill's

breathing changes as the attention she is getting is

beginning to change from the idea of a chore to

excitement. She tries to pull her feet apart so he can rub

between her legs, but her feet are still trapped in the

underwear. She tries to remove her foot without

disturbing her boss, but she takes too long and his

attention switches to the problem.

John bends down, continuing to rub on Jill's ass. He

uses his free hand to move the panties trapped around her

foot. With the panties being close to free, she pushes her

foot out, catching the toe of her black dress shoe on the

underwear band. The tension of the waistband maximizes

as she stretches her leg. John uses his thumb to unsnag

the panties. Jill loses her balance as the leg is thrust out.

She slides back six inches, face planting John right into her

moistening pussy.

Chapter Eleven

Embarrassed, Jill tries to quickly move her body forward to reposition her breasts back to their original location on the desk. John slides his rump rubbing hand around to her hip and clutches the other hip with his free hand. He prevents Jill from moving forward as he pushes a little harder into her pussy with the perfect view of her anus as the cheeks spread open around his face.

John's mouth opens wide separating the lips around Jill's clit. His tongue slides out from between his lips. His tongue glides up and down in a slow gradual motion from the tip-top of her clit to the luscious hole of her vagina. Jill quickly relaxes from embarrassment as she rests her head onto the desk. She begins to breathe heavily and let out an occasional moan as John applies a little more pressure with his tongue. She pushes back against the long deep strokes of his tongue. John takes his right hand placing it behind her right knee.

John applies a little force upward on Jill's leg. Without thinking about the action, Jill lifts her leg onto the desk. The repositioning of her body catches the bra holding her breasts on the desk. The nipples pop out of the bra easily. One of her breasts falls off the desk and out of the bra as she finishes repositioning. John reaches up with his left hand massaging the exposed spillage of the breast and nipple. He releases the kneading pressure of his massage as he initiates a clockwise rubbing of Jill's nipple. Jill moans as the contact with her nipples creates the climb to her peaking.

John begins rubbing Jill's leg with his right hand. Jill begins to bounce back and forth in a two inch pattern. Just as she is approaching the best climax she has had in over a year, the sun reflects in through the door. A car passing by attracts her attention. Jill realizes she can see Tonya walking up from across the parking lot.

"Quick, stop!" Jill has a panic attack realizing she does not want to actually be caught, "Tonya is coming!"

John pulls back looking towards the door. His hands drop down to grip his pant waistline as he jumps up from his knees. He runs into the office quietly spewing forth obscenities. Jill stands up quickly putting the papers back in order she was laying on. She glances down at the floor seeing a color shift as she moves her foot. She lifts her heel, lifts her toe off the ground, and slips the foot forward slowly. She quickly pulls the foot back, leaving the evidence of dislodged panties under Tonya's desk. Jill walks across the room to her own desk, standing in front of it. Tonya walks in the door setting off the laser dinger.

Jill smiles as Tonya walks around the corner, "Hi Tonya, how are you today."

"Hi Jill," Tonya pauses staring at Jill, "So, what's with the new getup? I have never seen you wear anything close to it before. It is definitely a good look on you."

Jill tilts her head with a nervous half smile, "Well thank you."

"You may want to consider getting a new bra though. Your nipples don't fit in that one, which isn't a bad thing." Tonya nods towards Jill's chest as she widens her eyes and raises her eyebrows with a sexy smirk.

Jill looks down at her nipples sitting out. The right is barely past the bra, but the left is out wide with almost the entire breast from the massage. Her face turns red. She turns towards the wall and begins the task of putting away her large hardened nips. Tonya giggles softly as the door to the office opens. John steps out observing the mortified look on Jill's face. He shifts to the pleasantly excited look on Tonya's face.

"Hi Tonya, what are you doing here on your day off?" John keeps his focus away from the mortified Jill for fear of ruining this day.

Tonya continues to watch Jill adjust her breasts in the mirror, "I have to meet a friend in the park shortly, and "I just thought I would swing in and grab my paycheck. I can come back later if you need me to."

"No, I don't have any further clients until after lunch." John steps back into his office, grabbing an envelope on his desk.

He hands the envelope to Tonya who seductively waves to Jill, "Nice to see you Jill. I like the new you. It makes coming to work ever so much more enjoyable."

"You too Tonya," Jill glances over her shoulder as Tonya disappears around the wall.

Three Women, Two Days, and a Night

The ding sounds as John steps back into his office. He grabs his car keys, dropping them into his pocket as he closes the office door behind him. Jill finally gets her bra back on properly.

Jill looks at John disheartened, "I'm sorry. This is too much. She saw my breasts. I don't think I can do this anymore."

"Why? This works for me. Tonya didn't seem bothered and I doubt she will say anything to anyone else. I do think we should stop long enough to get a bite to eat. I'm starving." John smiles holding out both arms wide and bent at the elbows.

Jill's embarrassment turns to anger, "Tonya seeing me naked works for you? And what, taking me to some cheesy restaurant will cure it?"

"I meant your look. Not to mention the fun we were having. I have to say I am enjoying it." John drops his arms to his sides and matches her disapproving facial expression, "You don't have to if you don't want to. You came to me, remember? You wanted more adventure in your life."

Jill drops her angry look, switching to an apologetic, "I know. I'm sorry. It was just really embarrassing. I do like getting the attention. And, it was kind of exciting to have Tonya admire me, but not something I think I want to go through with just anyone."

"Then it's settled. Nothing between us will change and today we go to your choice of restaurants." John grins as he steps forwards reaching around Jill for a handful of squishy ass.

Jill smiles unsure of why the boss is so attracted to her, "I was thinking the Japanese Steak House."

"After you my little strumpet," John holds his left hand out to gesture towards the door.

Jill bends over the desk grabbing her purse from the other side. John leans over slightly to admire the view of her ass as it lifts into the air when Jill rocks onto her

toes. She looks at John with a sexy smirk as she passes by

him on her way to his car. John follows two feet behind all

the way out the door with a strange grin upon his face as

his eyes never leave her backside.

John opens the car door for Jill as she gets into his

modest priced sporty sedan. He closes her door and walks

around to the driver's side. The car vrooms to life. They

head straight for the Japanese Steakhouse on the other

side of town. The car ride is silent with playful glances

going back and forth as the beginning of the day dances

within their memories.

The restaurant is only about half full. Jill and her

boss get put in a corner booth looking over the majority of

the restaurant. The grill in front of the little eighteen inch

table rim radiates heat. The seats are soft and foamy on

the bottom and firm on the back. Jill shifts a few times

before looking over at John. John is staring at her breasts

spilling out of the top of her bra. The areolas of both

breasts are visible above the bra. John scoots in closer,

getting a better view.

Chapter Twelve

Jill grabs the third button down, quickly putting it back in the hole as the chef walks up, "It's a better option then trying to fix it or having him stare at them while we are trying to eat. Plus, I don't want to share them with the entire world. You understand, right?"

"I understand, just as long as it doesn't become permanent. I would so hate to miss out on the new you." John laughs just before the chef introduces himself.

Jill sits as the chef pulls out little bits and bobs from

a cooler under the grill. The flashy style of cooking with flipping knives and bouncing spatulas makes a spectacle to see. Jill begins to laugh and enjoy the conversation between the chef, John, and herself. She forgets the whole embarrassing, yet tantalizing event with Tonya. Watching John attempt to use chopsticks provides an extra bit of fun and laughter. Luckily, none of the food he drops lands on her.

Jill looks at the table across the restaurant by the kitchen entrance. She recognizes the woman who ran into her earlier in the day. She watches as a woman in a very short skirt stands in front of the redhead with legs spread shoulder width apart. The redhead leans forward, placing her hand on the woman's knee. Jill bumps John to direct his attention without notifying anyone else by using an eye glance and slight head nod.

John and Jill watch as the redhead's hand slides up the woman's leg and disappears into the woman's skirt.

John reaches over to grab Jill's leg just above the knee. Jill grips his hand. She separates her legs as she pulls his hand up her skirt to feel the neatly trimmed, lost panty crotch. John rubs for only a moment before Jill releases his hand leaning forward. John returns his slightly moistened hand to the table top. John and Jill laugh, exchanging little dirty secretive glances. The chef leaves the table, thanking them for coming. John and Jill finish their plates of food. The meal ends with John paying the bill and leaving a twenty percent tip. The show and atmosphere in the restaurant worked in the chef's favor.

John and Jill get back in the car. Just as John brings the car to life in the restaurant parking lot, Jill gets an idea which feels a little crazy to her. Despite the feeling, she reaches over to the driver's side with her left hand. Her hand grasps firmly between John's legs. She rubs a couple times up and down before unbuttoning and unzipping his pants. A little careful negotiation, and the meaty snake pokes its head out of John's trousers. Jill looks at John who is gazing at her with eyes half closed and mouth halfcocked.

Jill begins to slowly jerk up and down as John manages to pull the vehicle out of the parking lot despite the pleasure he is receiving. Half way back to the office, Jill really gets into the little expressions and noises John makes as she plays with him. A little sticky fluid is forced out through the hole as she strokes up with a little firmer grip. She smirks at him just before they get to the stoplight. Her head disappears below the dash as she opens wide, extending her tongue half way out of her mouth.

"Oh my!" John's loud expression encourages Jill.

Jill pushes her head down until her head cannot go any further. John grunts with an ending moan. The car races a little faster as John extends his leg pushing on the gas pedal. Jill holds her head down as a warm fluid bursts from John into the back of her throat. She bobs up and down a few times to drain any excess fluid. She makes a smacking sound as her lips leave his cock. She smiles, remembering the pleasant taste of satisfaction. He releases the gas pedal with his hands going over each other to make the turn into their parking lot. Jill pulls her head up getting caught by John's arm. She bends down, sliding over before coming up. Her hand continues to rub on the spit covered rock. Jill spies a car sitting in the parking lot. She waves with her free hand at John's one o'clock appointment standing next to the car, Ms. McCrery.

John waves with one hand, keeping his thumb still hooked under the steering wheel. He quickly looks at Jill, catching her attention as she continues to rub. He looks down at his own big pulsating cock being jerked, over to Ms. McCrery, and then to Jill with a sexy playful grin upon his face.

"I don't think she would be interested in joining us, boss," Jill releases the hold on John and does up another button on her shirt.

John is slick as he slides everything below the belt back into place without shifting his upper body, "And I would never ask you for it. But, it can be a playful idea never acted on. Besides, you gave me the idea when talking about Tonya. You can't blame a fella if you put the idea in his head."

"Hello Ms. McCrery. How are you doing this day?" Jill laughs as she gets out of the car slinging her purse over her shoulder.

"I'm fine Miss Jill. At my age, there isn't any point in changing the things that can't be changed." Ms. McCrery heads towards the office door at a slow shamble giving time for Jill to pass her.

Jill unlocks the door, holding it open for Ms. McCreary and her boss. John directs Ms. McCrery into his office to hold the appointment on her investment

portfolio. Time passes on as Jill finishes the paperwork and

reads over emails sent to the company. Jill answers the

phone three times during the time spent reviewing the

emails. She schedules two appointments and cancels the

last one for the day. Ms. McCrery opens the office door

just as Jill begins to review the stock alerts. John escorts

the client to the door.

As John walks around the divider, he looks over to

Jill, "Been busy my sexy queen bee?"

"The last appointment for today has cancelled. The

emails have been addressed, but there are six you need to

review to make changes to people's portfolios. Two new

appointments are scheduled for next week. And, I did not

get to the stock alerts." Jill's gaze keeps a firm lock on the

boss's eyes.

"Sounds good," John stops inside the door frame to

his office, "I will need time to review the emails, but I think we are done for the day. Did you want to rendezvous at the hotel early? We can go straight there if you want."

"No, I need to stop by home first. My husband will need clothes for tomorrow and I need to throw them in the dryer. I can meet you there if there aren't any problems with me getting away for the evening." Jill collects her purse and the tote.

John walks over to Jill wrapping his arms around her with both hands firmly grasping her ass, "I hope there aren't any delays. I have been waiting for this moment since you started working for me."

Jill gives an odd looking grin. John lays a big kiss on Jill's lips. He relinquishes his grip and heads into the back office to finish the day's work. Jill triggers the ding as she exits the investment firm. The tote is slid onto her wrist as she uses the hand to find the keys buried in her purse. She double taps the button on the keyring to unlock the doors. She slightly pulls on the handle causing the door to pop open. A slight jerk causes the door to fly open rapidly because of the tilt of the pavement in the parking lot.

Jill climbs into the driver's seat after placing the tote in the back. Her purse is set on the passenger seat and she buckles her seat belt. She looks at the window to the investment firm. She produces a contented sigh as the ignition turns and the minivan putters to life. The drive home is a short twelve minutes with lots of music playing over the radio. Jill finds herself tapping her fingers along to the beat and singing the chorus lines. The day is changing her outlook on life.

The minivan pulls into the driveway of the ranch style house she has made into her family's home. She leaves the tote in the car as she makes her way to the front door. Without looking down, she switches between the keys on the ring with a single hand. The key goes into the front door lock. She jiggles the key up and down to get the deadbolt to unlock. Just one of the many things her husband has been unmotivated to do for the last three years.

She steps into the house dropping the keys and her purse on the little foyer table. She grabs a stack of mail brought in by one of her three kids. She flips through the mail. Finding nothing of interest, she places the mail back on the table. Her husband can deal with it when he gets home. She turns to the living room, pausing to look at the picture of her and her husband twenty years ago when she got married at the age of twenty three. She lets out a heavy sigh as she remembers the attention she received from him in the beginning of their lifelong relationship.

Chapter Thirteen

Jill walks through the living room to the master bedroom yearning for those days long ago. The fun they had back then. She sits on the edge of the bed as her mind wanders. The first date is always important, but for her, the first time her husband got to second base is the memory she treasures for the attention she now seeks.

They had just pulled into the parking lot of the university housing. The small talk was winding down and the nervousness in him deciding to try for a kiss was cute.

It was obvious as he tried to detect hints from her body language as he shifted his hands around while considering whether or not he should touch her. His eyes darting around, along with the hesitation, informed her he wanted to know how well the night went. He finally decided to lean in for the kiss on their tenth date. Although he had kissed her before, Jill believed he had intentions of trying a little more. Otherwise, why would he be so nervous?

Her future husband leaned over kissing her, keeping one hand above her shoulders and one on the side of her abdomen. Clearly he was showing respect, which she appreciated, but on this date she wanted more from him. After two minutes of kissing, she realized he was not going to make the first move. She decided to bait him into it.

"Let's move to the back seat," Jill pushed him back and spun around with her knees landing on the front seat.

Jill had already stuck one leg through the gap in the

seats before he knew what to say, "Okay, it is more comfortable back there."

Jill pauses as she straddles between the seats. She lets her knees buckle and her grip slip off the headrest. She falls, facing away from him, with a quick shout to declare a problem. He came to the rescue as expected. Both of his hands land on her then firm buttocks. She looks back giving him a wicked little smirk before jumping into the back seat. She decided to make it even more obvious as she removed her shirt and bra while he climbed into the back with her. Being topless in the back seat of the old Junker without a care, even as people passed by taking notice of the steamy windows was a turn on for her on that date.

Jill snaps back to reality and the loss of attention from her husband. She stands up, waiting next to the bed to see if any other memories come back to her. With only today's adventure coming into her mind, she heads to the laundry room. She pulls the laundry from the washer.

Most articles go into the dryer with the exception of a few

shirts hung to dry. She looks around the laundry room to

ensure nothing is missed. She heads back to the little table

in the hallway by the front door. She might as well head

over to the hotel to get settled in and wait for her lover.

There is nothing more for her here.

Collecting her things, she reaches for the

doorknob. As her hand comes to rest, a new memory

surfaces. The day he carried her across the threshold of

the hotel makes her relive her wedding night. Two years

after college, the night meant to represent the rest of their

lives together. What a glorious night it was indeed.

They had just arrived in their little suite at the

hotel. A quaint room with a little kitchen area, large

bathroom with two person tub, and a small balcony. Her

husband had picked her up outside the room and carried

her across the threshold. He tossed her onto the bed as he

stepped next to the king size mattress. Jill remembers

laughing wildly as he stepped back three steps and took a

running jump onto the bed. The bed springs were so

bouncy, he almost shot her off the edge and onto the

floor. They laughed for some time afterwards.

"What do you say we remove the dress, take a

bath, and have a little fun?" He whispered to her in his

deepest sexiest voice.

Jill rolled over onto all fours on the edge of the

bed, looking at him with her sexiest come get me look,

"How bad do you want it? If you want it bad enough, you'll

come take it."

That might have been the second fastest Jill's

husband ever moved, the first being when her water broke

three years later. While rolling up onto his knees, his shirt,

tie and jacket was pulled over his head and went onto the

floor. His pants were around his knees by the time he

moved in behind her. He grabbed the bottom of the dress

to pull it up over her.

"Not that easy!" Jill spreads her legs trapping the dress under her knees.

Jill's husband sucked in a loud deep breath, grabbing on either side of the back seam of her dress. He pulled the dress apart, ripping it next to the seam, from above her waist to six inches from the bottom hem. The cool air rushed in over her firm ass and trimmed pussy. Her husband exhaled abruptly in unexpected excitement as there was no underwear to impede him. Her arms gave way as the cool air tickling her receptive body meant it was finally time for her to feel him inside her. With all of the horseplay and sexual acts they had done over the years, he had never been allowed to stick it inside her.

Although the initial thrust caused a very brief moment of pain, the pleasure was intense as his long hard cock slithered in inch by inch. Jill reared back with her husband catching her in an upright, kneeling position. He pulled down on the top of the dress, ripping the front and allowing her tits to feel the cool air. The moaning and groaning lasted for almost an hour. The noise of the bedsprings echoes to this day in the halls of the hotel.

Jill jumps ahead to the bath where they talked of things to come. The first thing to come, despite not being discussed, was them on the balcony naked and wet with her husband bumping and grinding into her until the front office called with a complaint about the noise.

The thrill of almost being caught while making hard passionate love on the balcony is one of the vivid thoughts driving Jill today. She wants to find the passion her husband once had for her. She turns the doorknob, walking towards the minivan with a new adventure firmly planted in her mind. No sooner than closing the van door, her cell phone rings.

"Hello," Jill sounds happy despite the interruption in the new leg of her adventure as she clicks the answer button on the steering wheel.

The voice of her sister radiates out of the synced van speakers, "Hey Jill. Glad I caught you. We are still doing dinner tonight, right?"

"Oh, I completely forgot about it. I guess it is one of those days," Jill looks down at her wet crotch realizing she has no underwear on to soak up the moisture of the memories.

The voice in the speakers turns to a worrisome annoyance, "But, you can still make it, right? I want you to meet Jeff. You said you wanted to do this."

"Yes, I will still make it. I did tell you I would be there. So, he really that big in your life, Ashley?" Jill tries to remember what happened to her underwear but can no longer recall where she left them.

Ashley hesitates for a moment, allowing the line to sit silent long enough for Jill to check if she lost the connection, "I think he is. I am hoping he might want to take it to the next level and propose. But, I want your

input before I start dropping hints."

"What? You guys have been dating for six months.

Do you really think you know him that well? It is a big

decision and I don't want you to be unhappy down the

road." Jill forgets about the lack of panties as a motherly

tone comes to bear.

Ashley's tone changes to the annoyed independent

child who knows it all, "Now, I hope you aren't going to do

that at dinner. Maybe this was a mistake. You don't have

to worry you know. I will decide if he is good for me. I just

wanted your opinion, not make the decision for me."

"I know, Sis. I just worry sometimes." Jill starts the

minivan, "I will meet you at the Mexican restaurant at 5:30

tonight."

Ashley giggles with delight, "See you then. Bye."

Jill begins to say good-bye when she realizes Ashley

has already hung up. She looks at her phone shaking her

head. Her thumb taps the little yellow envelope. The thumb taps on the boss message chain from earlier in the day.

She taps out a message with both thumbs, "Forgot I had to meet my sister for dinner. Will meet you at the hotel after."

"Okay, will see you there. See all of you." The message, with a romantic attempt, comes back from John after a minute.

Chapter Fourteen

Jill reaches up grabbing the long black rod with

crowning knob. She pulls forward and down one step to

put the minivan into reverse. Turning around to look out

the back window, she pulls out of the driveway into the

street. She grabs the rod dropping it down two more

notches into drive. The van moves forward.

Jill drives towards the Mexican restaurant. She has

an hour before she needs to be across town, but she has

little time to do anything else before her dinner

appointment. She arrives at the restaurant with forty minutes to spare. She lets out a sigh as she looks both ways down the street before opening her car door. She grabs her purse and phone. The van door closes with a little squeak.

Jill looks at the door, "Just another thing to add to hubby's hopefully-he-will-do list."

Jill moves around to the sidewalk. She looks at the restaurant, deciding not to go in this early. She turns to scan the little shops nearby to burn some time. She notices her favorite little candle shop. Jill shrugs her shoulders in an unconscious reaction as she decides to go into the shop. The front door jingles as she opens the door. Jill scrunches the right side of her face, tilting her head and bringing up her right shoulder.

Jill doesn't mind bells, but these have a metallic scraping screech sound to them. The bells do not give a welcoming she prefers. Her face returns to a normal state as she breathes in deeply absorbing all of the inter-tangled scents. She is greeted by a young college man sitting behind the counter reading a mechanics magazine.

Jill wanders around the store for a few minutes before picking out a manly midnight outdoor scented candle for her sister and her new mystery man. Stepping out of the store after paying, Jill looks at her phone for the time. She still has twenty-two minutes. She looks at the store next door. Her eyes widen. A sex shop sitting next to her favorite candle shop. Jill squints wondering why she has never noticed this store before. She walks towards the front door. She glances around the street as her hand reaches for the door. The door flies open with Jill ducking in as quickly as she can disappear from the street.

Jill looks at the back of the store as the door to the office opens. The redheaded woman she saw at the coffee shop and the restaurant walks out into the store. She walks across the store and right past Jill. The redhead turns with a hand on the door.

"Aren't you the lady I spilt coffee on this morning?" The redhead tilts her head slightly with her eyebrows furled down.

Jill shifts her eyes from the left to right before focusing on the redhead, "Yes."

"I suggest the nipple clips," The redhead opens the door, "Nothing like a good pinch and pull. Have a nice one."

"Thank you," Jill watches as the redhead takes several steps away from the door.

The smell of sex fills the air around her as a voice comes from behind, "Can I help you today?"

Jill whips around in surprise, "Just browsing."

"Let me know if you need anything," the twenty year old woman moves over to a nearby rack.

Jill inspects the employee from behind. Her hair is messed up in back and a little tangled as if her hair was being pulled. The woman squats down with legs spread to grab a dildo which had fallen off the rack. Jill looks at her shiny wet almost oily spot sitting around her crotch on her jeans. The spot visibly grows as pressure is put on the pants from squatting down. Jill has discovered the point of origin for the sex smell. Jill turns to peruse the shelves realizing she should not be surprised as this is a sex shop.

Jill looks at her phone. Still has eighteen minutes. She looks over the odd variety of panties. Everything a person can imagine. Edible, scented, crotch-less, Velcro sides, and more on this one rack. She moves to the next rack finding a matching selection of bras for the underwear. Jill gives a half, left side, grin as she looks at a licorice bra. The sweat that forms under her large breasts would melt that bra in a minute or less. She moves on to the next rack. This is a large rack on the wall from floor to ceiling filled with a wide variety of nipple clamps and rings. The rack the redhead suggested for tonight.

Jill pays little attention to the rings as she does not have pierced nipples. She looks over the nipple clamps. She is unsure of the benefit of such a device having never had her nipples pulled or pinched hard other than breastfeeding her children. Her husband was always gentle with her breasts even when overly pounding her pussy. A few of the nipple clamp designs are attention-grabbing to Jill. She pulls three different nipple clamp packages down from the rack. She wonders if this would excite her boss, not to mention herself.

"That's not a bad choice," The clerk makes Jill jump slightly, "Would you like to try them before you buy?"

Jill looks down at the nipple clamps, "No, I think I will just get a pair."

"Not a problem. I see you as a dolphin person. But, if you open the package you can't return them." The clerk points to the dolphin shaped clamps in Jill's left hand.

Jill puts the dragon and star clamps back on the

rack, "I think I will go with the dolphins. I figured they could not be returned, but I don't have time to try them right now."

"Not a problem, but it would only take a minute. If you like them, you should consider getting your nipples pierced. I find it to be wonderful." The clerk points at her own nipples as if Jill can see through her shirt and bra.

Jill looks up from the shirt with a puzzled look, "Thanks, but I think I am a little old for such things. Plus, I need to get to a dinner."

"You are only as old as you want to be in your heart," The clerk takes the nipple clamps to the register as Jill follows, "I know several ladies older than you who have their nipples pierced. They all have active sex lives and always enjoy themselves. Only if you buy into the 'you're too old' idea are you too old, not to mention boring. Men don't like boring. Just a thought."

Jill pays for the clamps, "Thank you, but I don't

think the people I know would approve of such things."

"It is more important what you and your partner think about it than any stranger or friend. It may surprise you, but after the initial shock, they tend to like the idea or ignore it." The clerk gets in one last thought before Jill steps out the door.

Jill looks both ways down the street before moving from in front of the sex shop door. She hurries for the minivan before anyone can see her purchase. The side door opens, the package goes in-between the seats, the door closes.

Jill gets half a sigh out before jumping from the voice behind her, "Hey, you're a couple minutes early. Sorry about that, didn't mean to startle you."

"No problem, Ashley," Jill turns to find her sister snooping a foot away as she tries to look over Jill's shoulder into the van.

Ashley spins on her heels, "Jeff is inside getting us a

table. I thought I would come say hi before you decided to

bail."

"I wasn't bailing, just tossing something in the car,"

Jill glances back at the shut door of the minivan to double

check the invisibility of the nipple clamps sitting in the van.

Chapter Fifteen

Jill follows Ashley into the restaurant. A man at a table in the middle of the restaurant sticks his hand high into the air. Ashley bends her arm into the air at the elbow giving a quick wave of recognition without drawing attention to herself from other patrons. As Jill walks up to the table, she looks over her sister's boyfriend. He obviously has ten to fifteen years on her which is not a plus. A somewhat athletic build is a plus. The neatly done hair style is encouraging. Not to mention, he is wearing a sporty style dress jacket.

"Jeff, I'd like you to meet my sister Jill," Ashley grabs the back of her chair as Jeff stands to greet the ladies.

Jeff extends his hand across the table, "Pleasure to meet you."

"And you," Jill pulls her chair back after shaking Jeff's hand, "So, let's get the obvious question out of the way. How did you meet?"

Jeff smirks with a light chuckle, "Ashley rear ended my car with her runaway shopping cart. She felt bad and offered me a cup of coffee. There was no damage to the car and she was cute with her little worried dance, so I accepted."

"It was not a good cup of coffee, but he invited me to dinner after we choked the sludge down. It was magical." Ashley unfolds her menu to look despite only ever ordering one item from this restaurant.

Jill hands the candle over to her sister. Ashley opens the package, pulling out the candle. Jeff thanks Jill for the candle as it happens to be his favorite scent. The dinner continues with light conversation and the ordering of food. Turns out Jeff is a stock broker at a rival firm. He does seem a little mature for Ashley in Jill's opinion, but she is glad Ashley is happy. The fajitas for the table arrive and the conversation turns to remembering funny events in life as the food is depleted. The meal ends on a high note in the conversation as future plans and dreams are foretold.

Ashley walks Jill out to her minivan as Jeff settles the bill, "So, what do you think of him?"

Jill stops on the curb abruptly turning to Ashley, "He seems like a great guy. Two things I want to say, and I really need you to listen. First, don't jump in too fast. He does seem like a great guy, but take the time to know for sure. Second, if he is the right guy, don't ever let your love life get squandered. It is important to keep the love alive, especially through the awkward years."

"Thanks, Sis," Ashley gives a quick hand up wave as Jill walks around to the van door, "Will see you next week."

Jill returns the short wave before climbing into the minivan. The engine sparks and Jill pulls into the light traffic. She looks at the little digital clock on the dash as dinner took longer than expected. It is late evening, but she will still have time to make it to the hotel without being late for the original set time. She glides along the streets with little interruptions other than a few traffic lights. Pulling into the parking lot, she looks out the windshield at the four story building. It is one of the few sky scraper buildings in the town.

Jill opens the driver's door before grabbing her purse from between the seats. She taps her door closed with her left knee as she turns to the side door. She grabs for the side door of the minivan, opening it by giving a shove. She reaches in for the tote. She grabs the handle and begins to pull on the door when she stops, using her weight to keep the door from closing. She reaches in between the seats where the sex shop bag fell. She shoves it in the bottom of the tote and slams the side door closed.

Jill hits the button on her keyring to lock the van. She walks up to the side door of the hotel. Scrounging in the purse for a moment, she pulls out a white magnetic card with the hotel's logo on the front. She swipes the card through the magnetic card reader unlocking the hotel security door. The glass and metal door creaks as Jill swings it open as if the weight of the door is too much for the hinges.

Jill walks halfway down the corridor before she finds an elevator. The elevator arrives a minute after touching the slightly worn out green lit up button. The doors open with an overly dramatic slowness to them. Jill half expects someone to be standing in the elevator to

catch her going to her room without an alternative

explanation as to why she might be here. She steps onto

the empty elevator, relief showing with a light hearted

sigh. She looks at the panel of buttons on the inside of the

door.

The large silver metal panel only has eight buttons.

Four for upper floors, one for a basement, and one for

emergency, along with the open and close door buttons.

The panel seems overkill in size. Jill pushes the third floor

button. She looks up as if she can see where she is being

taken as her mind bounces between her current life and

the adventure she started this morning. A heavy sigh

comes from the conflicted mind of the married mother.

Her mind bats around the ideas killing the mood which has

been building all day. Is it possible to get back the

adventurous nature she had when she was younger? Is

this wrong at her age? Is this just wrong? Will society scorn her for her actions?

The elevator jerks as it comes to a stop on the third floor. The doors takes its time opening as Jill watches her reflection disappear with the widening gap between the doors. She steps into the hallway. The fake wood sign across from the elevator says to turn left. She pivots to the left, still wondering if she should be here. The pasty textured walls do not help convince her either way. The hotel room door is only three down from the elevator. She stands in front of the door for what seems like an eternity, although only a couple minutes pass on the universal clock. She inserts the card into the door as she decides.

The beep echoes in the hallway. The door handle is pushed down. The heavy door swings open. She steps into the little hallway leading to the room. Jill looks at the door to the bathroom on the left. The darkness filling the room means John is not utilizing the bathroom. She walks four steps to the edge of the hall. She looks around the room at the king sized bed, the mini fridge, and the TV on a dresser. Still no John.

The curtains moving, as a summer breeze blows in from the balcony, catches her attention. She catches a glimpse of John on the balcony before his hand grabs the side of the curtain. He pulls the curtain aside stepping into the room. He looks at Jill with a smile which quickly fades when she does not return the emotional gesture.

John sighs as Jill sets her things on the chair next to the dresser and turns to face him, "I need to talk with you, John."

"Did something go wrong with your dinner date?" John tries his best to grin, stepping closer to the bed.

Jill steps closer to the bed bringing her hands together in front of her, "No, it went fine. My sister has a good man in her life. I just don't know that I should be doing this. That we should be doing this."

"Why?" John's eyebrows raise as his head tilts.

Jill turns away from John, "I am too old to be doing this. I am a married woman who has settled into her life. This is just crazy. What will people think if they find out?"

"I thought you were tired of not getting attention from your husband. I thought you wanted to be young at heart. I thought this was your big break and you didn't care what people thought." John steps next to Jill putting his hand on the small of her back.

Jill pauses as John's hand begins to rub up and down her lower back, "Don't get me wrong, I do. I even enjoyed today at work. Although it was embarrassing when Tonya caught me with my nipples out, it was also exciting. But I don't think I can do this. Too many people won't approve if they find out. I don't want it to wreck my family."

"Well, if they don't approve it's because they are jealous. And you're right, work is probably not the best place for this activity. But, if this is what you want then you should do it. Besides, you did promise me. Try it one time with your heart in it, then you should decide for real what you want." John's eyes dart to the blank wall as he imagines a movie playing of Jill and Tonya looking at each other's breasts.

John steps behind Jill wrapping both of his arms around her as her head turns to look at him, "You are right. I will give it this one time. If it feels right after, then we can talk about more. If it doesn't, please don't be mad."

Chapter Sixteen

Jill tilts her head back as John comes over her

shoulder for the first kiss of the night. He puts his left foot

forward as their lips part, gently pushing on her to get her

to walk towards the bathroom. He walks with his arms still

wrapped around her, his steps going wide to prevent them

from tripping. He guides her right into the bathroom door.

John stops Jill from reaching for the light switch

with his left hand. His right hand grabs a long neck lighter

off the counter. Pulling the trigger, the lighter illuminates the large bathroom. He lights the three candles on the counter, each with two wicks. The bathroom flickers romance with the candlelight dancing on the reflective surfaces.

John continues to hold Jill's hand with his left to keep her from removing her clothes, "That's not what the boss wants. I get the pleasure of taking the clothes off this sexy body."

As the candlelight flickers with the smell of vanilla and lilacs filling the room, John sets the lighter on the counter and brings his right hand to the side of Jill's waist. The button covering the zipper head takes two tries to undo. The zipper comes down easily. The skirt falls around Jill's feet, exposing the bare flesh and lack of panties. John moves his hands to her hips. He rubs from the top of her hips down her upper leg and back again. His hands gravitate back towards the pudginess of her butt cheeks, but only stay for a moment before going back to her hips.

Jill reaches behind herself, finding the button of John's pants. The button comes undone quickly, followed by a snug tug to force the zipper to rip to the bottom. Jill rubs on the hidden prize inside his underwear as the pants get stuck just below his knees. John gives a quick assist to his underwear to unwrap the hidden prize for Jill. John steps in closer, forcing Jill to remove her hands from his cock. He reaches around her belly giving a gentle hugging squeeze.

Jill slowly breathes in, sliding her hands along her hips towards John. She stops just before reaching him. Curling her fingers, she applies pressure to separate her butt cheeks to allow the hardened rod to slip between them. John kisses on Jill's neck as his hands unbutton her shirt from the bottom up. His hands finish the last button before rolling up over her shoulders. Jill leans forwards to allow a gap between them to remove her shirt. She squeezes her cheeks together as she presses against his hips. John lets out a deep quick burst of breath as he pulls

her shirt down over her back. His hands press against her

back, rubbing up to the bra strap. His fingers dislodge the

tight bra allowing Jill to catch a deep breath.

John's hands move to Jill's hips as she remains bent

over with her breasts now bare to the flickering

candlelight. He firmly grips her thighs, thrusting his hips in

to press his hardened cock against her virgin anus. Jill

releases her deep breath as the sensual excitement pours

from her very soul. John steps back releasing Jill. She looks

back, a little puzzled. John rubs on her left ass cheek with

his right hand as he steps around her. He bends over to

start the water for the bath.

Jill sits on the toilet seat as John adjusts the water's

temperature. Jill watches John for a moment as his erect

penis refuses to move out of the way as he bends over the

tub to plug the drain. Without considering her actions, Jill

runs her hand over her leg to stop on the lips of her pussy.

Her legs spread wide, parting her lips and exposing her clit.

She watches John grab a scented bath salt container and

dump some granules in. She rubs up and down on her clit.

Her fingers slide down to the hole, barely sinking in. As her

fingers run back up to her clit, the entire clit becomes

soaked and lubricated with her excitement.

John turns to find Jill sitting on the toilet rubbing

herself as she stares at him, "Come here John. I want your

cock in my mouth."

John stiffens his body snapping to an upright

position. His body relaxes as a perverted grin forms over

his mouth. He takes two steps forward as Jill scoots to the

rim of the toilet lid leaning forward. Her right hand glides

through the air to meet the oncoming stiffened rod,

rotating it down towards her mouth. The two fingers in the

middle of her left hand surge deep inside her pussy as her

mouth engulfs the large cock. Jill presses forward on the

cock as she closes her eyes from the pleasure of her

fingers reaching maximum depth. Her face presses into his lower abs as she takes every inch into her mouth and down her throat.

Jill curls the fingers inside her easily with the immense juices flowing from her fully stuffed vagina. John's cock slowly slips out of her mouth as she moves her head back, placing her right hand at the base to keep it pointed towards her. She massages the bottom half with a moderately pressurized grip. The tips of her fingers meet the swollen soft skin of her g-spot. She moves her fingers in a counter-clockwise rotation as the cock finishes sliding out of her mouth. She pushes against the tip of the cock with her lips while continuing to massage the bottom half. The cock forces the lips apart, slipping back in till the tip finds the back of her throat as her hand flattens against his body.

While keeping the rotation going, Jill partially straightens her fingers to apply force down to give extra pressure to her already soaked crotch. John grabs the back of her head, running his fingers through her hair and occasionally rubbing the back of her head. She places her thumb on the top of her palm just between the middle and ring finger. The thumb is instantly lubricated. Her thumb slides up her vagina lightly and slowly until it finds her clit. Her body jerks slightly with the added stimulation. Her thumb presses down as her whole hand harmonically shifts in a counter-clockwise rotation.

As Jill's body gives a second little jerk, John pulls back. His penis snaps back upright to his body as Jill releases her grasp on the lower end. He looks down with the perverted smirk still on his face.

Stepping over the rim of the tub, John is mesmerized by Jill's fingers slipping out of her, "Not yet. The boss wants to take a bath first. Then we will see if we can release the wild and crazy lady within your heart."

"You are such a tease," Jill pushes lightly on her

knees as she stands up, leaving a glistening spot on the lid

and small trail going down the side as it glistens in the

candlelight.

John lays down in the tub with his legs spread

leaving enough room for Jill. She steps into the tub

squatting down. Her butt hovers just over his cock as John

stares at the adorable little anus, beckoning him in the

flicker of the candlelight. Jill's left hand moves between

her legs, grabbing John's pulsating cock to bring it to a

standing position.

John and Jill moan together as Jill drops her body

down allowing the entire cock to rapidly penetrate her

pussy. She flops back on him, her head landing on his well-

placed hand above his shoulder. Both of their legs

straighten together as the rising water envelopes their legs

and most of their bodies.

John shifts his hips up and down, moving his cock

in and out an inch. Jill moans again. His hands wrap around

her body. He slowly rubs up and down on the sides of her abs. She begins to rotate her hips forcing him to stop his hips movements. Her hands pass over his, going under her breasts and pushing the tits towards her face while her fingers wrap around to squeeze. His eyebrows bounce up once as the intensity of the show brings a surprise of erotic entertainment. His hips begin to move once more, this time to her rhythm. Her legs bend, emerging from the water and landing on the rim of the tub.

The hips slowly rotate a little less until a heavy sigh of contentment comes from Jill's lungs. She lays back on John enjoying his hand rubbing over the side of her abs and across her stomach. She closes her eyes, still able to see the dancing lights of the candles through her lids. John starts to hum a romantic melody softly into her ear. Although time seems to stand still, it is not long before his hands wander from their path and end between her legs.

Jill's eyes pop open as John's middle finger lightly

grazes her clit with his hips pumping his cock deep into

her. She gasps for a short, quick breath of air. Her head

turns to look at him. He raises his eyebrows with the

perverted smirk returning to his face as they come down.

The smirk shows on her face in kind as she sits up in the

tub. She grabs the side of the tub, closing her eyes and

tilting her head back as an extra inch of his cock pushes in

from the extra weight of her body.

Jill stands, allowing the cock to fall out of its perfect

pocket. She looks back at John. Her perverted smirk turns

to a playful grin as his lower lip puckers out in sadness. She

steps out of the tub. Her breasts hang down past the rim

as she bends over the tub with her hand gently gripping

his balls.

Chapter Seventeen

"If you want more, you'd better hurry up and come get it," Jill whispers in the candlelight.

Jill's hand runs up John's cock as she straightens up. She walks out of the bathroom still dripping wet. John springs from the tub taking a good portion of the water with him. The floor is dowsed as John's left foot slips three inches. Undeterred by the danger, he keeps moving to exit the bathroom. His cock bouncing up and down as if wagging with excitement.

Three Women, Two Days, and a Night

Jill is standing at the foot of the bed as John rounds the corner from the bathroom. He comes up behind her before she can get onto the bed. With both of them still soaked, his cock slips between her butt cheeks as he wraps his arms around her body. She tightens her butt cheeks around his penis giving him another unexpected stimulant noticeable by his rather loud gasp for air in her ear.

Jill lowers her upper body so her hand can rest on the bed. She lifts her left leg up and over the bed, almost completely straightening it. Her cheeks spread wide, allowing John to see her cute little anus and dripping pussy in the mood setting light of the hotel room. He backs his hips two inches and leans forward slightly. His cock runs down between her cheeks, catching on the upper rim of her pussy. She looks back at him, closing her eyes and opening her mouth in pleasure as he rams every inch deep inside her.

John brings his hands around. He curves his fingers

into her hips. He squeezes in on the fatty thighs, pulling back with his arms as every thrust of his hips tries to push her forward. Jill screams out in delight. Her arms give way, allowing her body to fall to the bed. Her left breast lands on her left hand. She begins to wiggle her finger to push-in on her nipple and move it around. Her right hand darts for her soaking wet clit. She presses with all four fingers, stretching the lips far apart and applying constant pressure between them. The hole of her vagina shrinks as the skin is pulled, causing the muscle inside her to grow seemingly larger. Her body tingles as she approaches her first multiple orgasm of the night.

Jill looks over at the sliding door to the balcony as a gentle summer breeze moves the curtains. She shifts her hand to hold her lips apart with the outside fingers as she uses her two middle fingers to rub hard against her clit. Her muscles stiffen as her back begins to arch. The muscles lining her pussy begin to constrict around John's cock. Her head tilts down as she screams into the mattress.

John's level of excitement triples as Jill has her multiple orgasm. He takes a deep breath and slows his thrusts down to be slow, going from the tip of his penis to as deep as he can muster. Jill's body shakes as a second multiple orgasm follows the first. She quickly releases her clit as the tingly sensation becomes overwhelming. She puts her hands over his, getting him to release enough of his grip to slide his hands off her hips.

As his cock pops free from the warm wetness, Jill looks back with the perverted grin forming once more, "I'm ready for you to cum all over my ass. Time for you to enjoy this as much as me."

"Trust me, I am," John has a weird grin on his face as Jill pulls on his hand to lead him onto the balcony.

Jill looks over the parking lot as she bends over the railing. Her breasts dangle just past the bars as she lifts her right leg to place it on the old lounge chair. John steps up behind her, pressing down on his cock with two fingers to get it into the right position. The tip slides in easily. He closes his eyes for a split second as the rest slowly slides in. Jill inhales slowly as the cock reaches its full depth.

John starts off slowly with full strokes in and out. Jill's soft moans encourage him as his speed begins to increase. She lets out a moan. He switches to deep thrusts, only coming out half way. She shifts her body and turns her head to the side. He watches as she sticks her middle finger in her mouth, coating it with saliva. Her hand reaches around her back with her finger landing on her cute little hole.

As she applies light pressure, she glances back at him, "I told you, I want you to cum all over my ass!"

Jill's middle finger applies enough pressure for the tip of her finger to enter her tight little hole to the end of her fingernail. Her head spins back towards the parking lot as she moans a little louder. John reaches through the railing and under the bar to grab her bouncing breasts, feeling the spillage of her breasts go between his fingers as he squeezes. His body leaning forward applies more pressure on Jill's finger towards the hole on her backside.

The extra pressure causes Jill to moan loudly as her right hand lets go of the railing with a direct line for her clit. John releases her breasts, snatching the rail on either side of her. His thrusts are short, deep, and fast. Jill's fingers press hard as she rubs her clit, she lets out a scream. She looks down into the parking lot, watching a couple getting out of the car. They look around the parking lot to find the location of the scream, but never look up.

John's arms tighten as he uses the leverage to thrust harder. Jill rolls her left foot onto the toes as she is lifted from the ground by his thrusts. Her body slides over the railing and the finger in her ass pushes in and up. Her breasts swing, almost hitting her face on the way up and slamming into the bars on the way down. She screams louder and moves her fingers in a large circular pattern as fast as she can over her clit and pussy lips. John begins to grunt louder and louder with every thrust. Jill screams as every muscle tightens from a multiple orgasm as John pulls out. Jill removes her fingers from her pussy and ass, grabbing the railing with both hands. John grabs his cock with his right hand, stroking as rapidly as his wrist can move. He tilts his head back with a loud grunt. White, creamy fluid shoots the inch from his penis to her anus. She feels it splatter over her anus. The fluid begins to run down towards her pussy as a second load lands on her left cheek.

Jill relaxes her body, spinning her head around to look at John as he sits gazing at her. She begins to straighten her body, moving her left hand around to rub over her ass cheek and anus. She smears his cum around as she gives John a satisfied, yet perverse smirk style smile. John grins from ear to ear. He sticks his hand out. She spins on her heels reaching out with her right hand. As he pulls her into the hotel room, she glances over at a low sound coming from nearby. She watches as a young college student's body twitches with her arm straightened and hand down the front of her pants facing Jill's balcony. Jill gives the young lady a little wave as she is pulled into the hotel room by John.

John spins around planting a long kiss upon Jill's lips. His right hand reaches around for the small of her back as his left hand wanders to squish the fluid free side of her ass. His penis, still mostly hard, presses against the lower part of her stomach. She reaches around planting both hands on his buttocks.

As they release each other, John turns to head for the bathroom with Jill following behind, "John, did you see the young lady on the balcony two over from us?"

"No, did she see us?" John uses his left hand to aim as he lets out a sigh and begins to urinate into the toilet.

Jill grabs a small hand towel from the counter to clean up her backside, "I would be willing to say so."

"Why?" John turns his head to watch Jill in the mirror with one eyebrow raised.

Jill shrugs slightly, "It looked like she enjoyed the show."

John laughs as he steps around Jill. She sits on the toilet as he moves to the bed. Jill sits for a moment before she is able to let the flow out. She wipes and walks into the room to find John laying under the covers of the bed slightly propped up on the headboard.

Jill turns and tilts her head slightly, "Are you staying the night?"

"Well, no one would miss either one of us if we were gone for a single night. Do you really want it to end without a little romantic attention by cuddling?" John flips the covers over on the empty side of the bed.

Jill walks over to the bed, crawling under the

covers, "True. My husband isn't supposed to be home until tomorrow. It is nice to have the extra attention."

"Then I would say that you are happy with our arrangement. I know for a fact the wild side came out in force." John puts his arm around Jill pulling her over to him.

Jill scoots in, placing her head on his shoulder as he places his hand on her breast, "Yes, the wild side did come out. If this continues, I may want you to cum in my ass instead of on my ass. I'm glad we did this. I really needed the release."

Jill closes her eyes, falling into a satisfied, content, gratified sleep. John sits watching her for a short period of time before reaching over and turning off the hotel lights.

Chapter Eighteen

A brunette hair woman walks out of the coffee shop, stopping on the edge of the sidewalk. She takes a sip of her mochaccino and squints upwards at the sun bouncing off the few surrounding sky scrapers a block away from the shop. She takes one step closer to the curb just as a red headed woman coming from across the street tries to slip past her to avoid a bike messenger whipping by with little regard to the pedestrians and motorists.

"Ow," The brunette hair woman switches hands

holding the mochaccino as hot liquid spills on her thumb and down the back of her now free hand.

"Sorry, the bike messenger came faster than I thought he would," The red head watches as the brunette haired woman shakes the hot liquid from her burning hand.

The brunette haired woman curls one side of her mouth in a sexual mannerism, "It's not a big deal. Happens from time to time on my own. Even this can't ruin today."

The redhead walks to the large window of the coffee shop. She pauses for a moment, glancing down at her watch. She turns, looking back at the brunette haired woman. The brunette haired woman is already across the street, rummaging in her purse for something. The redhead turns back around to look in the coffee shop window once more.

The redhead turns away from the coffee shop. She walks briskly, yet with a comfortable demeanor and stride.

At the corner, she turns left heading down a dead-end street. Almost at the end of the street, she turns towards a small apartment complex of eight units. The building itself is a beige color with dark Mark Twain red trim and doors. The redhead looks at the button name plaque on the right side of the door as she steps onto the front porch. She finds the button for the Swanson residence and pushes, holding the button down for three seconds before releasing.

"Yes," A voice calls out in a robotic tone over the cheap speaker, "May I help you?"

The redhead leans towards the speaker and microphone slightly, "Yes, this is Ruby Red. We have an appointment."

"Yes," The voice drops off unsure about the idea, "I will buzz you in."

The door buzzes with a loud clink noise as the electronic deadbolt shifts to allow entry. Ruby grabs the door, pulling it open an inch before the buzzing stops. The door swings open rather easily and holds itself open as Ruby steps through. The entry way is decorative in style with three apartment doors visible and a mailbox setup on the right. The stairs on the left in the middle of the hallway prevent the fourth door on the main level from being seen.

Ruby heads up the wide stairs with the funky blue vinyl flooring. The hallway at the top of the stairs mimics the look downstairs without the mailboxes. Ruby looks at the nearest door, reading the number seven centered on the wood at eye level. She turns to the right, taking five steps to the door with the number eight. She raises her hand to knock as the door opens.

A man stands in the doorway, "Hello Doctor Red. I'm Charles."

"Glad to meet you Charles," Ruby opens her fist turning the knock into a wave, "May I come in?"

Charles sidesteps swinging his arm towards the inside of the apartment to gesture Ruby in, "Glad to meet you. My wife is in the living room."

Ruby walks into the quaint apartment. She notices Charles stiff stance and the reluctant look upon his face. She smiles at him as she walks by. Charles musters a half-ass smile back towards her. Ruby walks into the living room to find the wife sitting on the couch. A chair from the dining room is positioned to face the couch. Ruby sits in the chair, leaning forward and extending her hand.

"Hi, I'm Ruby Red," The husband sits on the far side of the couch as the wife shakes Ruby's hand.

The wife sits back mashing her fingers together, "I'm Carole. I don't really see why we are meeting here. I'm not sure we really need an appointment."

"You wanted the appointment," Charles leans back putting his elbow on the arm of the couch and his fist against the side of his forehead.

"Well, it is important for us to meet here so both of you will feel more comfortable as you open up," Ruby places an elbow on each arm and interlocks her fingers, "And by what I have seen so far, you do need a little help. There isn't any shame in it. If there was, I wouldn't have a job. So, let's begin by telling me a little bit about yourselves."

The room is awkwardly silent for a moment before Charles leans forward, "I'm Charles. I work construction and handyman jobs around the city. I do a little bit of online selling on the side to make a little more money."

"I'm Carole. I am a stay at home mom. And, now I feel like I just joined AA." Carole sighs heavily with embarrassment and contempt.

Ruby smiles as she observes both of their posturing, "Most introductions are like that though, right? I am Ruby Red, a sex education therapist. I put the red in love and the ruby in the bedroom. I'm curious what you want to get out of therapy."

"I think our love life is fine. It was just a spur of the moment to try this. I'm not really comfortable with this. I am too old to be doing this, and what about our daughter?" Carole turns to look directly at Charles.

Charles looks down with a low moan, "Yep. I figured. Sorry to have wasted your time Doc."

"Please, call me Ruby," Ruby sits back in the chair unlocking her fingers and putting her hands on the arms of the chair, "And, you aren't wasting my time. You are wasting yours. Obviously you need help. There is no such thing as too old and your daughter knowing there is a sex life after getting married isn't a bad thing either. It is better for her to think she should wait for sex until later in life. Having sex too early can cause problems."

"I don't want my daughter to know. And I am fine with our sex life." Carole leans forward flaring her nose and lowering the tone of her voice.

Charles sits up straight turning towards Carole, "What sex life? We have sex if you are in the mood. You decide what and how. You decide where and when. You are only interested once every three or four months. You don't even consider what I want or need. There is nothing of what I like or don't like. That isn't a sex life. And, our daughter is reaching sexual maturity. If she thinks sex is something before marriage, we can expect to be grandparents early in life. Not to mention, her husband will probably divorce her."

"And what? We should go with what you think? I should do things the way you want around here? You have all the control anyways. And, I don't intend to discuss masturbation or sex with my daughter, she is too young." Carole stands up facing Charles as her voice becomes loud enough to hear next door.

"Okay, let's settle down for a minute," Ruby leans over, reminding the couple there is another person in the room, "I know it seems embarrassing, but this is actually good. You made a quick breakthrough. Most people take months to get to this point, but that is why I do this in the home. I have a question, are you ashamed of your body?"

"What? Why?" Carole sits down stiffening her back and turning her head slightly to the right with a puzzled look upon her face.

"The way you dress and handle yourself, the things that were just discussed, and the way you two interact tells me you are ashamed of your body." Ruby's tone turns pleasant with a blank peaceful face, "I just want to ensure I am not wrong."

"I am not ashamed. I just think the body shouldn't be flaunted everywhere. It should only be seen in the bedroom." Carole uses a religious school teacher tone.

"I see," Ruby closes her eyes as she nods, "And what do you think about this Charles?"

Chapter Nineteen

Charles sighs as he knows the problems the truth will cause for him all week, "I think it is a load of crap. She can't get past her past or what everyone else thinks. She is so wrapped up in what others might think that she is ashamed of her body. I want her to go back to when we were first married and knew the body isn't a bad thing. It not only causes problems for us, but also for our daughter."

"That makes sense," Ruby continues despite the

scoff from Carole, "The body is not something to be ashamed of. You should respect others when leaving your home or inviting them over, but other than that, the body can be flaunted without issue. I have an idea for another breakthrough. Carole, I want you to take your shirt off."

"I don't think so," Carole places her arms over her chest squirming in her seat.

"Why not?" Ruby points to Charles as he adjusts the rising pinch in his pants, "It obviously is an idea which excites Charles."

"Yeah, because you are in the room," Carole drops her hands to her lap glaring at Charles.

Charles sighs as Ruby laughs, "No, Charles is excited because he is going to get to see your breasts. If you are not ashamed with your body, it shouldn't be a big deal. Would it help you cope if I did it too?"

"My husband doesn't need to see your breasts!" Carole's face turns a flush red, "I can't believe you would even suggest such a thing! And I am too old to be walking around half naked!"

Ruby leans forward ever so slightly, "I understand. I want to point out something to you. Did you know in many states in the US and several countries around the world, it is legal for a woman to go around topless? Also, you are religious which dictates you are trying to get closer to God. Doesn't it say in the bible that Adam and Eve only covered themselves after they sinned due to shame? Then wouldn't it hold that to get closer to God one must become more comfortable and find no shame in being naked?"

"What?" Carole takes a long pause with the red fading from her face, "I'm too old for such nonsense. Well, I don't know. I would have to think about it. Besides, there are so many perverts in the world."

Ruby smiles, "True. And you cannot be responsible for anyone other than your family. So, since time is almost up, I would like to propose something for the two of you to work on for the next week. Carole, you will show your breasts to Charles for a minimum of two minutes a day. He can stare at them, play with them, or play with himself while touching your breasts. For this week, you decide whether or not there is sex following the show. But, you cannot do it at the same time every day and you can't do it in a stacking timetable."

"A stacking timetable?" Carole raises one eyebrow while moving her hands to hold her belly.

Ruby accents her words with hand motions, "Yes, today you show him your breasts after I leave. Tomorrow you show him an hour later than today, and so on. You need to be spontaneous with your times."

"I guess I can do that. But what if my daughter catches us?" Carole pulls her hands up making the hefty E cup breasts lift two inches.

Ruby gestures rotating both palms to an upward

position with a slight widening of her arms, "Then she will know you guys love each other. It isn't like you are having sex in front of her."

"Okay, I will try for a week." Carole slightly drops her shoulders as she gives in to the idea.

Ruby turns to face the eternal grin of Charles, "And for you Charles, you will give your wife a hug and kiss every night before you go to bed. You must tell her you love her, and there is no grabbing or groping of butts, breasts, or anything to be defined as sexual."

"Okay?" Charles's face scrunches up for a moment, "I can do that for her."

Ruby stands, grabbing her purse as she rises, "Then I will see you both next week at the same time."

The couple thanks Ruby and gives a goodbye. Ruby shows herself to the door. She turns around to grab the open door handle and sees Carole lift off her shirt as Charles drops his pants. Carole's breasts are already part way out of the bra as she reaches behind her to unstrap

the slightly smaller than her breasts piece of clothing.

Ruby closes the door. She proceeds down the stairs,

heading out the front door with a good work smirk on her

face.

Ruby strolls towards her car parked past the coffee

shop. She stops just as she passes the barber shop to look

in the coffee shop window. She shrugs her slender

shoulders before turning towards the door. She walks into

the coffee shop. There are a few patrons with two baristas

working. She saunters up to the counter. She orders a

latte, watching the barista carefully as she makes the

beverage.

Ruby pays for the latte, taking the takeout cup for

the door. She pauses as her hand lands on the metal bar to

push the door open. A tiny sip of the hot beverage hits her

tongue. She winces as the heat irritates her tongue from

the burning sensation. She pushes the door open and

walks towards the curb. The little white man appears just as she reaches the curb.

Ruby crosses the street, turning to her right. She stops at the corner waiting for the red hand to turn into a little white man so she can cross again. She blows into the little hole on the lid of the cup in a hope to cool the latte slightly. The white man appears again. She crosses the street, but turns before she reaches the other corner.

Walking down the street on the driver's side of the parked cars, Ruby reaches the back end of her car just as a car turns the corner at too high of a speed. The car comes close to hitting her. She jumps behind her car, spilling her latte all over the trunk. She turns to curse the driver, but hesitates as a sound from the car screams about a stupid dog.

Ruby watches in horror as a small black dog is held outside the passenger window with the car barely slowing down. The female hands drop the dog four cars down from

Ruby. The dog yelps as it hits the pavement, rolling to a stop at the back end of a tire. Ruby runs for the dog, screaming obscenities at the vehicle until it disappears around the corner. Ruby sees small spots of blood on the street before reaching the dog. She whips her shirt off, leaving only the see-through lace bra on.

Ruby bends down to look at the dog. It is a small breed with clumps of hair on its head, feet, and tail. The black skin gives her only a moment's pause to wonder what the owners had done to this dog to make it lose its fur. The dog looks over at her as she reaches her hand to scoop the poor animal into her arms. She lifts the dog a couple inches off the ground before it yelps and starts a whimpering cry.

Ruby slides her shirt under the dog before pulling it the rest of the way out. She lifts the dog, holding it nestled against her breasts. She looks around for anyone who will make eye contact with her as she races for her car. Most people are whispering and pointing, but no one will come

forward as she tries to get their attention. Finally a young

woman of sixteen years walks up to the opposite side of

her car as Ruby places the dog in the back seat.

Chapter Twenty

Ruby straightens up and closes the car door as she listens to the young lady, "That was horrible. I am glad you helped that poor dog. Did you know you're naked?"

"I still have on a bra, but it doesn't matter as it is perfectly legal for me to be topless. Where do I find a vet around here?" Ruby glares at an older woman scorning her lack of shame.

The young lady points in an imaginary line through a building, "I know of a vet two blocks down. They are good. It's where my parents take our dogs."

"Thanks, got-ta go," Ruby jumps into the driver's

seat, allowing the car to roar to life without getting

situated.

Ruby pulls the car part way into the street without

looking. A honking horn causes her to step on the brake.

She looks down the road before pulling out a second time.

She reaches for her seatbelt after taking the first left to get

to the vet. Two blocks down, she sees the sign for the vet.

She pulls the car into a parking spot, slamming on the

brakes hard to stop. She scares two people walking on the

sidewalk. She ignores the people gesturing as she

apologizes to the dog for the rough parking job. Ruby gets

out of the car, retrieving the dog from the back seat

before crossing to the vet's office.

Ruby bursts through the swinging door, "I have a

medical emergency. This dog needs help."

"Okay miss," an older lady looks at her from across

the counter, "Do you have an appointment? And what is the dog's name?"

Ruby gently lays the dog on the counter, "Not my dog. Someone threw it out of a moving car in front of me, so I brought it here."

"I know it sounds heartless, but we don't usually take in dogs like this. Usually people go to the animal shelter for help with these situations." The lady looks at her see-through bra raising both eyebrows slowly.

Ruby looks at her crossly, "I will pay for the dog's treatment. I will be collecting the dog after you fix it. And don't comment on my breasts. I am not in the mood right now."

"I understand, I was just going to suggest we switch your shirt for a blanket. You look a little cold. I will get the doctor." The lady pulls a blanket from under the counter and places it next to the dog.

Ruby pets the dogs head as it lays on the counter.

The dog seems to be spaced out from the pain and intense situation. She carefully unwraps her shirt laying the dog on the blanket. Before she can wrap the dog, the vet walks out into the lobby.

"Don't wrap your dog, I need to be able to take a look at it," The female vet nods at Ruby before turning her attention to the dog.

Ruby begins to put her shirt on, but stops as she notices the blood and smells the distinct odor of urine, "So, what can you tell me, Doc?"

"Hello little one. I am going to just check you over real quick. It seems there is no internal bleeding. There are scrapes on the body. The left rear leg is broken, but it is just a hairline fracture. Oh, you poor thing, you lost a tooth. That explains all the blood." The vet talks her way through the exam as the puppy whimpers to help calm Ruby, "It is a female. About eight months old. And based on her size, a runt of the litter."

Ruby rubs along the bra line of the yellow lace sports bra, "So, nothing you can't fix, right? How long before I can pick her up?"

"Yes, we can set things right. It is lucky. We will hold onto her until tomorrow afternoon. You can pick her up then." The vet smiles at Ruby as the dog is gently taken to the back room by the assistant.

Ruby is handed an information card by the vet. She fills it out before thanking the vet and leaving. Ruby steps outside and looks around the street for a moment. She sees a cut-through to enter the park. She considers it for a moment. Deciding she could use a little time to let the adrenaline out, she crosses the street and cuts through the buildings to the park. The sun feels good upon her skin and the summer breeze relaxes her as her nipples get excited.

Ruby crosses to the far side of the park before calming down and realizing where she is walking. She turns down the main walkway to get back to her car. A woman starts to walk by in a pink low cut jersey knit top and dark blue jean micro skirt. The woman stops to gawk at Ruby's B cups sitting almost bare in public.

Ruby turns to the woman, but cannot get any words out before the woman steps forward and points at Ruby's chest, "I love the look. That yellow mesh lace bra is a nice summer look for you."

"Thanks," Ruby stops to rethink her plan of attack.

The woman steps a little closer with a sexy smirk forming on her face, "Personally I don't like bras. I think they are too restrictive."

"Those are nice. Maybe you would like to grab lunch? I know a great Japanese Steak House." Ruby's day improves as the young woman lifts her shirt flashing her breasts to Ruby.

The woman lowers her shirt, "I have to go by the store to grab stuff for dinner tonight with my parents, but I can do lunch first."

"My car is this way. I will drop you off at the store afterwards. My name is Ruby Red by the way." Ruby points towards her vehicle on the other side of the park.

The woman begins to walk with Ruby, "My name is Kate. So, you're not worried about running around without a shirt on?"

"No, legally you can be topless anywhere a man can be topless. I have a spare shirt in the car for when we go into the restaurant." Ruby looks over at a pair of women walking by the fountain glaring at her.

Ruby and Kate walk to the car parked across from the vet. They are chit-chatting about clothing and the nice summer weather. The drive across town is smooth through traffic as Ruby explains the dog odor in her car and the events leading up to her being in the park. As Kate listens, she keeps watching Ruby's breasts bounce as the car goes down the road. The car pulls into the Japanese Steak House. The restaurant is busy, but not packed. Ruby pulls out a spare shirt from her trunk before going into the steak house.

Ruby and Kate are taken to a table in the corner upon Ruby's request. Kate sits across from Ruby. The chef comes out to the table and pulls different little starter treats from the fridge under the grill in the center of their table.

Kate looks at Ruby, "So, why invite me to lunch?"

"If I meet someone new who interests me, then I prefer to ask them to a meal to get to know them better. You never know, we may be a good chemical mix. But a better question, why did you agree to lunch with me?" Ruby begins to eat the appetizers the chef puts in front of her.

Chapter Twenty-One

Kate takes a bite and waits until after she swallows, "Well, to be honest, I'm not sure. You see, I use to see both women and men. Due to the pressures I get from people around me, I stopped seeing women. I have been thinking about it a lot recently, and I believe I want a romp with a woman."

"Makes sense. So, you thought it might be me?" Ruby points to an item on the menu for the chef to make.

Kate points out her meal preference to the chef,

"Maybe, but I don't know. I haven't been with a woman in a while. Your breasts are smaller and perky. It gave me a rush to see them today. I am thinking with my hormones, not my head."

"It doesn't hurt to think with your hormones from time to time. Since you aren't young, I see no problem with you deciding to have a romp. You are not saving yourself for marriage. Or, are you married?" Ruby looks deep into Kate's eyes awaiting a response.

Kate holds the eye contact with Ruby, "No, but I do have a serious boyfriend. I am just not sure that I want to share him with another woman. It isn't something I am prepared to do just yet."

"Two things to consider. First, would you be willing to try it out for a single night to see if it something you want? Second, why are you afraid?" The chef passes out the food and excuses himself to go to another table.

Kate begins to eat a delectable lunch, "I am afraid

he would run off with the other woman. And, if we ever get married, I don't think it would be right for him to have another partner. I wouldn't have another guy after I get married. And, I don't know if I want to try it out or not."

"Well, there is a big difference from having two guys in a relationship and having two women in a relationship. But, I don't think we should get that psychological and theological on our first lunch date. But to decide on a tryout, is the idea that society frowns upon such things keeping you timid?" Ruby switches from chopsticks to a fork to continue eating.

Kate looks up with a giggly laugh, "I don't put much stock in the rules society lays out which make no sense. Just like I don't wear a bra, I don't wear underwear either. I think it is too restrictive, and I love the feel of my bare skin. The occasional breeze titillating my nipples and clit is something I don't ever want to be without. And anytime I want sex, a man needs easy access to my body."

"No panties, huh? I have a way to decide for you whether or not you should give tonight a try. Come over here for a second." Ruby sets her fork down, turning towards the edge of the seat facing the aisle.

Kate sets her fork down. She hesitates for a moment, pondering what Ruby might be doing. She stands and steps over to Ruby. She turns to face Ruby with a strange look upon her face as the quizzical nature of a surprise might bring. Ruby reaches up, placing her hand just above Kate's knee. She slides her hand up Kate's leg and under the skirt. Ruby grabs Kate's pussy, squishing the puffy bald lips together between her thumb and three fingers with her palm up. Ruby's pointer finger hits its holy mark at the back of Kate's pussy. A rush of fluid runs down the finger. Kate closes her eyes, sucking in a deep breath and holding it. The pointer finger runs from the hole, between the pinched lips, and straight to the clit.

Ruby glances over to see the woman she spilt

coffee on this morning watching her. Ruby brings her hand back, pulling on the pussy lips until the puffy lips roll back into place. Kate releases the pent up air from the top as she releases additional fluid down below.

"I would have to say," Ruby looks at her sopping wet finger, "You could really use a trial. I would definitely go for it. But you do realize it would not involve love?"

Kate looks down at Ruby's wet hand before returning to her seat, "I think you might be right. But, why would it have anything to do with love? I just need some loving, not love. Why, are you suggesting I stop by your place tonight?"

"Normally I don't do one night stands, but in your case I would love that. I have something special I would like to introduce you to. Also, I think I would like to find out how adventurous you really are." Ruby finishes her lunch before jotting down her address on a napkin.

Kate finishes her lunch and accepts the napkin, "I

am plenty adventurous enough. I will be there after I have

dinner with my parents."

"Good, and we will see. I look forward to finding

out what you know and are willing to take." Ruby drops

some money on the counter for the bill.

Kate stands up next to her, "Don't know what you

think I haven't done."

"Don't mail out a check your ass can't cash. I know

more about pleasing a woman than any woman should,

with exception to Dr. Ruth of course. You still need a ride

to the grocery store?" Ruby smiles as she turns towards

the door.

Kate giggles, "Yes, I still need to head to the store."

Ruby walks out the door followed by Kate. The

dynamic pair get into Ruby's car whose dog odor has faded

as the back windows were left cracked. Discussions vary

from the dog to what Kate's parents are having for dinner.

Occasionally Kate tries to figure out what Ruby has in mind

for tonight. Ruby seductively dodges all of the sexual questions Kate asks. Ruby suggests the only way to know is to show up.

Ruby stops in the parking lot to drop off Kate at the grocery store. Kate leans over giving Ruby's perky B cup a good squeeze before getting out of the car. Ruby pulls the car away from the curb. She looks down at the time before going into a panic. She is going to be late for her afternoon appointment. She believes she is rushing across town, but is actually neither moving faster nor is actually behind for any work related appointment.

Ruby gets to her next personal appointment. The large parking lot is mostly empty as usual for this time of day. The lunch crowd has left and the few people who come in after are not looking for the attention of a large crowd. Ruby pops the trunk after parking near the front door. She walks back and pulls a small duffle bag out. She looks down at the dirty shirt sitting in the trunk and remembers she no longer has a clean one to switch into. A single laugh escapes as she considers working out in just her sports bra.

Ruby looks at the big neon glowing sign as she walks to the door. Bard's Gym, a twenty four hour gym and the only gym in town. She pulls the front door open. She steps in and scans the floor. Betsy, the two hundred and fifty pound lady, is sitting on a stationary bike directly across from the equipment for toning the groin muscles. Randy, the hundred pound man, is doing a stair step aerobics routine. Shasta, The lady of the night with clothes too small for her braless rack, is doing light free weights. Then, of course, there is Carl. He has been working here since day one of the opening. Ruby has been trying to find out why such a sweet, polite man works here and has no girlfriend.

Ruby walks to the front counter with just a hint of sway in her hips as she considers Carl agreeing to be her exercise equipment today, "Hey Carl. So, anything new in life?"

"No, just the same old routine for the most part," Carl looks up from his muscle magazine, "My mother seems to be doing better this week. I guess that could be seen as a new blessing. But, she does have to stay overnight at the hospital for some kind of monitored test."

Ruby grins as her eyes open a little wider, "So, that means you have tonight off. Nice to know."

Chapter Twenty-Two

Ruby raises both eyebrows as she looks the muscular man up and down in an obvious fashion. She pulls a magnetic strip card out of her duffle bag, swiping it on the little card reader by the monitor. As she walks towards the changing room, she glances back and catches Carl checking out her hot body.

Ruby enters the medium sized locker room. The smell of sweat mixes with the different perfumes of the shower products the women use after working out. She walks down the side of the lockers, looking down each aisle to pick one out. She reaches the third of five aisles when she sees a familiar face. Turning down the aisle, she admires the heavy set, enormous breasted woman with legs spread straddling the bench. She can't help but be drawn in by the strawberry blonde hair. The woman's areolas are the size of small side plates and has a large pussy one could lose themselves inside for the rest of their lives.

Ruby sucks in a breath and holds it for a second, "Hey Rhonda. How did your workout go?"

"Not bad. Think I pushed myself a little too hard today though. I feel wiped out." Rhonda says with heavy breaths.

Ruby faces a locker in front of Rhonda, opening the door and setting her bag inside, "I warned you last week not to push too hard. If you aren't use to working out, it can hurt more than it will help."

"I know. I think I just need a rub down. Then I'll be alright. Maybe I will see if the massage parlor has an opening." The heavy breaths continue to come out of Rhonda.

Ruby takes off her shirt before turning to Rhonda, "You want me to give you a quick rub to get you past the pain?"

"That would be great, but I don't want to interrupt your workout. Just let me sit for a minute and I should be alright." Rhonda leans forward trying to stretch her back, but breathing heavier.

Ruby pops off her shoes and pulls down her pants, "You really should stay sitting up with your arms up. You might pass out. I wouldn't want to see that happen to such a nice lady."

"Good point. No one wants to have to pick my fat butt off the floor. But my arms are too tired and sore for me to keep them up." Rhonda sits up, watching intensely as Ruby takes her string thong off.

Ruby removes her see through sports bra before walking behind Rhonda, "Nothing wrong with your fat ass. Personally, I would like to become better acquainted with it. Here let me help you."

"Thanks Ruby. You sure it isn't a problem? Not to mention me still being wet from the shower." Rhonda leans back against Ruby's bare skin as Ruby lifts her arms.

Ruby cradles Rhonda's elbows in her own as she begins to rub down Rhonda's arms, "Wet, sweaty, and naked is how I like the ladies who nurture my libido."

Ruby rubs down Rhonda's arms and onto her shoulders. Rhonda relaxes a little. Rhonda's forearms bend in, allowing her hands to land on Ruby's breasts. Ruby drops her rub down onto the pectoral muscles as Rhonda starts to gently move her fingers to rub on Ruby's nipples. Ruby drops her hands to rub from the underside of Rhonda's breasts up to her shoulders. Ruby bends slightly every time her hands go down, pushing her breasts into

Rhonda's hands.

Rhonda lets out a heavy sigh, followed by a quick

deep breath as Ruby pinches her areolas, "I could get use

to this after every workout. But, I do need to get to work,

not to mention I need attention in more places than just

my boobs."

"You available for dinner this weekend? I would

love to have you over. We could discuss things in more

detail." Ruby lowers Rhonda's arms as she sits on the

bench behind Rhonda.

Rhonda looks down as Ruby runs her hands over

Rhonda's belly and onto her upper leg, "I can make time.

You have my number, just give me a call."

Rhonda bends over as she straightens her legs with

her hands still on the bench. Ruby gets a wicked perverted

smirk on her face as Rhonda's butt cheeks spread. Ruby

can see the enticing star of an asshole between the

cheeks. Ruby slips her right hand between her own legs to give her clit a quick pass just to keep her thoughts together. Rhonda steps over the bench to the opposite side of Ruby's locker. Ruby leans forward slightly reaching out her arm and giving the fat ass a good squeeze. Rhonda looks back and smiles before sitting down facing the locker to put her underwear on.

Ruby moves to her locker, pulling out a solid color pre-formed sports bra and a pair of shorts. Slipping the clothing on in a quick fashion, she says a quick goodbye to Rhonda. Ruby enters into the gym again. Carl watches Ruby walk over to the bench press kitty-corner to Betsy. Betsy nods at Ruby as her routine slows on the stationary bike. Ruby adjusts the weights of the bench press machine before laying down on the bench.

Ruby begins to press the weight. The first set goes easy enough. Ruby realizes that Betsy is staring at the leg opening of her shorts. Without underwear and with the loose shorts, Betsy has a good view of her pubic region.

The second set is a little more trying. Ruby tilts her knee out, giving a little better view for Betsy. Ruby can hear the bike start to pedal a little faster. The third set is trying as Ruby's chest muscles are knowing they are being worked. Ruby holds the last repetition up for as long as possible. As the bar slowly drops, Ruby lifts her legs giving the ultimate view to Betsy.

Ruby looks over as she hears a commotion. Betsy is leaning to the side with one foot on the ground. Apparently, Betsy's foot slipped off the bike pedal as she became a little too excited over the show. Ruby smiles, giving a little finger wave to Betsy. Betsy smiles, glancing around the room at any unwanted attention. They both see Carl heading over their way.

Carl steps to the side of Betsy, "Are you okay? Any injuries?"

"No, I'm fine. I just got a little too excited." Betsy

shifts her eyes over to Ruby's shorts as she thinks about the excitement.

Carl glances over to see what Betsy was looking at, "Try to be careful."

Carl's eyes open wide as he sees through the large leg hole of the shorts. The bald pussy holds his attention for a moment. He turns as Betsy nods, giving an mm-hmm without looking him in the eye. Carl adjusts his pants as he walks back to the front desk. Ruby puts her head back down on the bench for a minute as she thinks about Carl and Betsy enjoying the show.

Ruby rolls her back as she sits up on the bench. She switches over to the groin toning machine. A quick pull and push of the safety rod adjusts the weight to Ruby's desired selection. She sits down on the machine while Betsy gets back on the bike.

Ruby puts one leg into each stirrup with legs spread. She shifts over three inches in the seat in order to be centered on the machine. She doesn't realize the shift

has slid her loose shorts to the side three inches, allowing

her spread vagina to be open to the public. Ruby pumps

out the last two repetitions of her third set when she

notices Betsy is staring without pedaling the bike. She

glances down to see what has mesmerized Betsy. She lets

out a single quiet snort of a laugh through her nose before

dismounting the machine and moving to the abdominal

machine next to it.

Betsy gets off the bike, heading into the locker

room. Ruby looks over at the clock as she finishes her abs.

She has been here already for an hour. She decides to

work out on one more machine before hitting the showers

and doing some shopping for tonight. The set on her

calves goes quickly. Ruby waves at Carl as she heads to the

locker room. Carl waves back just as Ruby's hand hits the

locker room door.

Chapter Twenty-Three

Ruby walks past the first isle, seeing Betsy sitting

on the bench nude with a towel over her stomach as if she

is waiting. Ruby turns down the third aisle. She stops in

front of her locker, noticing Betsy from the corner of her

eye go by to the showers. Ruby pulls the sports bra band

on the bottom out and up. The band catches on her left

nipple piercing, giving it a good pull and flick. Her nipple

becomes hard in an instant. The bra is tossed into the

locker along with the shorts. She grabs a towel from the

rack at the end of the aisle. She can hear Betsy start the

shower as she gets to the ornate off-white tile doorway.

Ruby looks over the half wall and sees Betsy sitting

on the other side on a bath bench with the shower water

sprinkling over her body. Ruby gives a quick greeting,

proceeding to the open bay shower station two down

from Betsy on the same wall. Ruby pushes the shower

bench in her station against the single wall with the

showerhead. She plays with the controls until the

temperature becomes slightly hotter than warm, but not

too hot to burn. Betsy leans back against the half wall,

watching every move Ruby makes.

Ruby squirts two shots of shampoo from the

dispenser on the wall into her left hand. She closes her

eyes as she begins to rub the shampoo into her hair.

Scrubbing for two minutes before rinsing off, she can feel

the mix of water and bubbles running down her body and

over the piercings on her breasts. She wipes away the

excess water in her eyes. Opening her eyes, Betsy is watching her with her left hand on her nipple and her right hand going under her stomach and between her spread legs. The right side of Betsy's mouth has a slight curl.

Ruby gives a quick smile before reaching her left hand out to the body wash dispenser. A single squirt lubes Ruby's palm. She rubs her hands together to get a slight lather. She wipes her left hand over her shoulder down the top of her right arm and back up the bottom of the arm. She gives the armpit a good lather before switching to her other arm. She rubs the wiped on body wash into her skin on both arms before reaching for another shot of soap. She does a light lather before placing her hands above her breasts. She slowly runs her hands over her pierced nipples. Her hand start a circular motion over her breasts, giving a rising and hardening sensation to her nipples.

Betsy watches intently. She spreads her legs as far as she can spread. Her whole arm begins moving up and down to allow her fingers to rub on her clit. As her arm

moves, it jiggles her stomach making her right breast

jiggle. She pinches, pulls, and twists her left nipple. As

Ruby soaps over her stomach, Betsy begins deep short

breaths.

Ruby turns around to face away from Betsy. She

sticks her right leg onto the shower bench on the wall as

her right hand reaches for a squirt of soap. She bends over

with her ass cheeks spaced, pointing directly at Betsy.

Ruby uses the soapy hand to rub around the inside of her

thighs before bringing her hand straight down the middle.

Ruby rubs back and forth several times as Betsy begins to

moan.

Ruby glances back at Betsy as Betsy's arm is jiggling

the fat of her stomach and extra-large breasts. Without

straightening up, Ruby reaches around. She runs her hand

straight down the crack of her ass. She gives a few short

strokes over her anus, watching as Betsy begins to twitch

her legs. Ruby puts her foot from the bench onto the tile shoulder width apart. She runs her hands over her back cheeks with her body slightly bent. She quickly bends over at the waist, running her hands down the back of her legs. Her hands wrap around to the front as they go up with both hands smacking into her crotch.

The echoing, popping smack sound is all Betsy needs for her big finish. She opens her hand, filling it with as much of her left breast as she can. She makes a fist with her breast being pinched in her hand. She pushes in hard, enveloping her hand with breast. Her right hand pushes in for maximum pressure on her clit. Her arm stops moving, but her body continues to jiggle as it convulses from the orgasms. She lets out a grunting moan just as the orgasms subside. Her entire body relaxes as her left arm falls next to her on the bench and her right lays on her leg.

Betsy's eyes pop open wide as she realizes Ruby is walking over, "I'm so sorry. I don't know what came over me today."

"Actually, I'm flattered." Ruby walks around the half wall, stopping as Betsy averts her eyes.

Betsy sits with little trembles going through her legs and body, "I really don't know why I did it. It isn't like me."

"Think of it this way," Ruby leans over the wall to whisper to Betsy, "If you would be willing to come on a regular basis to exercise and get healthy, then I would be willing to shower for you. It isn't something I oppose, and you shouldn't be ashamed since I am willing to participate. I come here two to three times a week. I'll see you Monday."

Betsy turns to watch as Ruby walks out the shower door, barely being audible, "Monday then."

Ruby stops next to the dirty towel bin to dry off. She drops the towel in the bin as she makes her way to the locker. Opening the locker, her exercise shorts fall out onto the floor. She grabs the shorts with her toes, bending

her leg to retrieve them without having to bend over. Her

left hand pulls the unzipped duffle bag from the locker.

She places the shorts in the bag along with her sports bra

she wore when exercising. The thong slips on smoothly

over her legs. She uses her left hand to slightly spread her

butt cheeks, pulling on the panties with her right hand to

set the string in its proper position. She looks down at the

see through lace front, happy with how cute the abstract

floral design looks with her bald skin showing through.

Ruby pulls the see through lace sports bra over her

head, setting her breasts inside the cups. She gives her

piercing a light flick with her index fingers turning them

into rocks. She takes a deep breath reaching for her shirt.

Pulling on the shirt, she thinks about the poor puppy

sitting all alone in the vet's office. She sighs deeply as the

mood waivers, knowing it is only for one day. The

distraction of the dog trips her up as she tries to put on

her pants. She tips, falling over and ending up in a sitting position on the bench. She laughs as her feet emerge from the bottoms of the pants. Standing up, she pulls the pants up and fastens them into place.

Ruby collects her belongings. With Betsy still in the shower, the walk out of the empty locker room seems mundane. She looks around the exercise room to find the entire place deserted, with the exception of Carl at the customer reception. She walks across the large padded floor room, stopping at the front desk.

Ruby leans her forearms onto the counter, "So Carl, you are going to come over tonight, right?"

"I don't know if that is a good idea. I don't want to impose. It has been a long time since I dated anyone. You know, with my mom being sick." Carl looks up imagining the show Ruby performed earlier.

Ruby can see the smut look in his eye, "I am not asking you to date me if you don't want to. What do you say you come over tonight, I have a surprise that will rock your world. If you enjoy tonight, maybe we can discuss dating. It never hurts to give it a dry run at our age."

"I guess I could, but I am still unsure if I should be coming over. This kind of thing really isn't me. I'm not a dry run kind of guy." Carl sets his magazine down, getting up from the padded stool.

Ruby stands up straight, lifting both shirt and bra to expose her pierced breasts, "You aren't married. Neither am I. Are you sure you wouldn't want a chance to play with these?"

"Yeah, I will be there," Carl's wide mesmerized eyes stare at the unblinking nipples, "But, what surprise?"

Ruby places the bra and shirt back into place, "You show up tonight and you'll find out. I am sure this will lead to many deep discussions about our future relationship. See you then sweet thing."

Chapter Twenty-Four

Ruby gives a wave over her shoulder as she exits

the gym before Carl can object or change his mind to

tonight. The short walk to her car is exhilarating with the

added bounce in her step. She has been trying to catch

Carl's eye for two years now. Throw in another woman

coming over, and it is triple the fun. The trunk slams shut

after dropping the duffle bag inside.

Ruby whips through the almost empty parking lot.

She starts to pull left onto the street when she hits the

brake again. She spins the wheel all the way to the right, pressing the gas pedal half way down. Her car glides over the pavement towards a little shopping district. She pulls her car over to the right, parking along the curb in front of the only sex shop in town. She bounds from the car to the front door.

"Oh, hi Ruby. How are you today?" A disheartened voice from behind the counter finds its way to Ruby.

Ruby turns to see a melancholy clerk, "What's the matter, Michelle?"

"Oh, just been thinking a lot lately. I do love my fiancé, but I am just wondering how good life is going to be. It is kind of ironic, I work in a sex shop, but I have never had an orgasm. I just don't know if Billy will ever be able to satisfy me." Michelle looks down at the counter while rubbing a single finger back and forth across the glass.

Ruby tilts her head slightly to the left, "You never? Not even by yourself?"

"I tried that, but it didn't seem right and kind of hurt a little. Besides, I always thought if I needed it, then I could just find a guy to do it for me."

Ruby chuckles, "And how has that been working out? Sometimes a person needs help for the initial, but seldom does it work to just have some guy who knows as much as you do, do it for you. If you would have explored your body earlier in life, then you could do it yourself."

"I know," Michelle sighs as her eyes briefly roll towards the sky, "Now you sound like my parents. They always said better to explore yourself than to have a stranger do it for you. Billy has done a lot to me, but nothing seems to work."

Ruby drops her chin slightly with her cheeks curving in and eyebrows raising, "That is actually not a bad saying. So, you said your man has done a lot. Tell me some of the stuff he has tried."

"We have tried several positions. Him on top, me

on top, and even doggy style. He has played with me countless times. I play with him more than he does me, but I know he likes it more than I do." Michelle looks through the glass countertop as if able to see the memories as they run through her mind.

Ruby looks up and to the left as she thinks, "Has he ever just forced you over the kitchen table, oiled you up, and crammed every inch into your ass?"

"No, he is too gentle for that, and although he wants too, I know you shouldn't be doing stuff like that. It isn't proper." Michelle's eyes fix on a single point.

If it is something you like and something he needs, why not? You do need to communicate about those things before trying it though. But, as it turns out, I can help. I was just going to look for something new, but this will be fun to do."

"What are you thinking of doing?" Michelle freezes in place, bringing her gaze up to Ruby.

Three Women, Two Days, and a Night

Ruby walks over to the vibrator section of the store. She looks through the selection. A smile forms on her face as her hand picks a point at a spot on the wall. Ruby grabs the vibrator and signals for Michelle to follow her into the back office. Ruby holds the door open as Michelle walks past her into the office.

Ruby drops the vibrator on the desk, "We need batteries for this."

Michelle picks up the vibrator with her right hand. She pops the battery compartment off the end with her left. She finds two 'C' batteries in a little basket on the shelf above the desk. Ruby reaches around Michelle as soon as the battery compartment is tightened on. Her left hand grabs a bottle of oil sitting on the desk. Her right hand grabs the vibrator. Michelle looks nervously at Ruby over her shoulder.

Ruby uses her thumb to snap the cap off the oil, "I want to see that pussy of yours. Drop your pants and let's see how good this vibrator really is."

Michelle silently unbuttons her pants. Just as the top of her butt begins to show, she stops pulling down her pants. Ruby leans in, setting the items in her hands on the desk. Her hands come back, hooking the top of Michelle's pants. Ruby forces them down enough to expose Michelle's entire ass. Ruby's hand runs back up Michelle's torso. Ruby's fingers slip under the wireless bra and displace it enough to crudely free Michelle's tits. Ruby cups the bra band burnt breasts with massaging hands.

Michelle breaths deeply and relaxes. Ruby leans into her. Michelle is forcefully bent over the desk. Ruby slides her hands back down to the pants. She squats behind Michelle as she pulls down, forcing the zipper apart as the pants scour against Michelle's hips and ass. The pants stop falling at Michelle's ankles. Ruby retrieves the oil from the desk while still squatting behind Michelle. She squirts a large amount of oil just above Michelle's crack.

Ruby's right hand delves into the oil, spreading it from the top of Michelle's crack to the tip of her clit. Michelle's hairy crotch and ass glisten from the coating of oil.

Ruby squirts another large amount of oil into the palm of her right hand. The palm presses against Michelle's clit and rubs backwards. Oil drips from the long pubic hair and Ruby's hand as a rhythm is formed. Back and forth with firm pressure. Michelle begins to moan. Ruby continues to rub, but angles her hand so only the fingers make contact. She squirts another shot of oil into her palm. The palm presses against Michelle. Ruby's hand runs from Michelle's clit to the top of her ass crack as Ruby stands up behind her. Large drips of oil fall from Michelle's bushy pubic hair into her underwear below.

Ruby steps to the left side of Michelle, reaching over her with her right hand to grab the vibrator sitting on the desk. She sets the oil on the desk in front of Michelle. The vibrator comes to life as Ruby turns the little dial on the end. Ruby sets the vibrator on the small of Michelle's back. Michelle moans a little louder with expectation of what is to come. Michelle sticks her hands up her shirt, playing with her own breasts. She massages her tits in a semi-violent manner as Ruby slides the vibrator overtop of Michelle's ass.

Ruby turns the vibrator so the miniature penis shaped tickler is pointed towards Michelle's clit. With all of the oil applied, the vibrator slips right into Michelle. Ruby only sinks it deep enough to lightly touch the tickler to Michelle's clit. Michelle mms in response. Ruby pulls the vibrator back until the tip just comes out. She reinserts it slowly until the tickler puts a little more pressure on the clit.

The third pull and thrust causes Michelle to moan as she lays flat on the desk still holding her breasts. Ruby harmonizes the movements a little faster. Michelle bends her knees slightly with every new thrust, trying to get a little more inside her. As Michelle grunts, Ruby slips the

vibrator out to the tip, spins it around to face the tickler

up, and reinserts the vibrator until the tip of the tickler

rests against Michelle's butt hole.

Chapter Twenty-Five

So enthralled with the experience, Michelle doesn't think about where the tickler is placed. Instead, she just enjoys the sensation as she lets out a combination of moan and grunt. Ruby pulls the vibrator out to the tip, sliding it back in slowly. Michelle bends her knees to insert the pleasure rod in faster and deeper. She lets out a gratifying scream as the penis head of the tickler is fully submerged into her ass. Three more thrusts and the entire tickler is deep within to Michelle's enjoyment.

Three Women, Two Days, and a Night

Ruby switches her harmonic movements to short deep penetrating thrusts. Michelle lets the sounds of pleasure and sex come forth with little pause to breathe. Ruby reaches her left hand around Michelle's leg. Ruby uses her index and ring finger to spread apart the hairy lips. Her middle finger presses hard against Michelle's clit. Ruby rotates the finger in a counter-clockwise manner. Michelle brings her arms in towards her body and her hands to her chin. Her leg muscles tighten. Her toes scrunch in her shoes.

Michelle tilts her head up to face the wall as her face and neck muscles tighten. Her butt clenches the vibrator in the deep position. Michelle lets out an enormously rewarding scream as her body ventures to the realm of orgasm. Ruby lets go of the vibrator, which stays firmly in place as Michelle orgasms.

Michelle's entire body relaxes all at once. The vibrator slowly slides out of her pussy and ass. Ruby grabs the end of the vibrator just as the tickler falls out. Ruby

sets it down on the desk, causing the desk to vibrate from

being left on. She steps to the other side of the office,

dispensing a handful of sanitizer into her palm. She grabs a

towel, wiping off the sanitizer. She turns, leaning over

slightly as she notices the dripping of oil and cum from the

hairy bush of Michelle.

"You should keep that. It is a good tool. Also,

consider telling your fiancé to play with your ass. Using the

vibrator in your pussy and on your clit while he pounds

your ass will work every time." Ruby watches Michelle's

movements enduringly.

Michelle hears the office bell ding to tell her

someone just entered the store, "Oh no, someone's here.

What do you mean play with or pound my ass?"

"You have a real anal fixation need. Trust me, you

love it. I will greet the customer on my way out. Have a

good day, sweetie." Ruby opens the office door, stepping

out onto the showroom floor.

The brunette haired woman she saw at the coffee shop and the restaurant is standing in the store. It as if this woman has a twisted mysterious fate to Ruby. Ruby's expression of disbelief fades quickly as she remembers three times in a single lifetime is not such a big deal. Ruby walks across the store and right past the woman. Ruby turns with a hand on the door.

"Aren't you the lady I spilt coffee on this morning?" Ruby tilts her head slightly with her eyebrows furled down.

The woman shifts her eyes from the left to right before focusing on Ruby, "Yes."

"I suggest the nipple clips," Ruby opens the sex shop door, "Nothing like a good pinch and pull. Have a nice one."

"Thank you," The woman watches as Ruby takes several steps away from the door.

Ruby pauses at the curb to look around. A

satisfying day half over. The lack of people on the street as

it nears dinner is a little puzzling, but she laughs the

strangeness off. It has been a different sort of day today.

The car roars to life. Ruby makes a beeline for her house.

Dinner must be done and over before her guests arrive for

dessert.

Ruby hits the little button on the roof of her car.

The large black iron gates of her filthy rich family style

home creek and grind as they open. Ruby leaves the gates

open as she is expecting the two guests to arrive soon

enough. She parks her car in the driveway near the front

door. She looks over the estate as she exits the vehicle.

The thought of the little puppy have such a large yard to

play in brings a comforting smile to her face. Ruby enters

through the right double door in the front of her house.

Ruby makes her way to the kitchen. She pulls out a

cutting board and a knife, setting both of them down on

the counter. She pulls a small pot out of the cupboard,

setting it on the gas stovetop on the island. She measures

out the water into a measuring cup. The bag of rice gets

poured into another measuring cup, but only half of the

amount compared to the water. She mixes both together

into the pot. She grabs a bottle of soy sauce from under

the island, spritzing in enough to add a little flavor to the

rice.

Reaching into the fridge, she pulls out carrots and

celery. She scrapes off the skin of the carrots by dragging

the blade of the knife across the length of the vegetable.

The carrots and celery are chopped into thin slices. She

pulls a large skillet out, placing it on the gas stovetop. She

turns the heat to medium high. The cans of mushrooms

are pulled from the pantry and drained of juice. She chops

the stems and pieces into little fragments.

With the pan now hot, Ruby puts two tablespoons

of butter into the pan. A spatula is used to spread the

butter over the pan. She dumps the carrots and celery into

the hot butter. Half way through sautéing the vegetables,

she scrapes the mushrooms from the cutting board into

the mix. The spatula stirs the mixture to a fine blend.

Ruby uses the soy sauce, Greek seasoning, and

seasoning salt on the vegetables to increase the delectable

flavor of her meal. As everything finishes cooking, Ruby

transfers the contents of the skillet into the pot. Stirring

everything together, she serves herself a gourmet oriental

style vegetarian dish. She sniffs the vapors coming from

the plate. With a spirited sigh of indulgence, she grabs a

fork. She moves to the next room to eat her favorite meal.

The large walnut table with seating for twelve sits

in the lavish dining room. Ruby makes her way to the end

of the table. She sets her food on the silk placemat. The

large dual arm dining chair makes a scuffing sound as she

pulls it back. She sits down, scooping up her fork with her

right hand. The first bite enters her mouth. She closes her

eyes as she holds onto the flavor of the morsel. As her

eyes open, she begins to scoop and chew. Four bites pass

before she removes her eyes from the round antique

metal frame of the clock on the wall between the elk head

and the bear head. Time has escaped her and her guests

will be arriving soon.

Ruby collects the dishes as she finishes eating. She

deposits them into the kitchen for the staff to clean

tomorrow. She runs up the left side of the curved ballroom

stairs visible from the foyer. At the top of the stairs, she

hangs a left. She goes into the first set of bedroom doors

directly in line with the top of the stairwell. She walks past

the ornately carved walnut king sized bed and straight into

the oversized walk-in closet most people would call

another bedroom.

As soon as Ruby passes the closet doorway, she

strips off a piece of clothing with every step. Standing in

the nude, she slowly rotates around to look over the

clothing hung on the racks. She selects out a sleeveless, V-neck, open belly, denim shirt. It looks raggedy, worn out, and old, but in fact this is the first time she has worn it since buying the shirt last week. She lifts her arms, allowing the holes to slide down her arms. She does up the three buttons on the front and straightens the little hanging wings going down the sides of her belly.

Ruby rotates slowly again. She reaches to a small shelf and grabs a pink, floral lace, see through thong with a string back. Stepping into the thong one leg at a time, she starts her rotation again. Her eyes fall upon a slinky pair of stone washed denim shorts with a brown leather belt. She examines the oval topaz jewel design for a moment. She nods, bending down to step both feet into the leg holes before pulling the shorts to her waist. She tilts her head, spying a pair of knee high black leather boots. She grins as she grabs a pair of calf socks off the shelf with her left hand and the boots with her right.

Chapter Twenty-Six

Ruby bounds onto the bed, not waiting for the bed

to stop bouncing before putting on the socks. The boots

slide on and she zips up the sides. A little hip thrust gets

enough momentum to bounce her to a standing position.

She overdramatically swings her hips with each stride out

of the bedroom. She laughs to herself half way down the

stairs. She walks to the front door, peering out the window

next to the door for any early arrivals. With no one in

sight, she walks into the living room. She bends over at the wooden wine rack. She hums until she is able to decide on the perfect year for tonight.

She sidesteps to the marble top table next to the rack. The cork takes a little effort to pull, but as she breathes deeply with the pulled cork next to her nose, she knows she has chosen wisely. She pours the entire bottle into an aerating decanter sitting on the table. She grabs three wine glasses from the hanging rack above the table. She sets them down in front of the decanter. A step back to examine the scene, and all is right for the events tonight.

Ruby hears the car pull into the driveway. She looks across the room at the clock. Her first guest is a little early, but this will give Ruby the chance to ease into the night. She heads to the front door, opening both doors just as Kate walks up.

"Hello. I wasn't sure if you would be coming on time. I know dinners with the parents can run late. I'm glad you are here though. The night wouldn't be the same without you." Ruby steps to the side to allow Kate to enter.

Kate pauses in the foyer, taking in the majesty of the house, "This is your house?"

"Only for the summer. I saved a portion of the money from my book sales to rent it for three months. It comes complete with staff. I was always curious what it would be like to be rich and famous. Now I know." Ruby closes the doors, gesturing Kate to the living room.

Kate steps into the living room, "That sounds like a wonderful idea. My family owns a house like this on the other side of town. My parents only give me small amounts of money every month. They say I need to learn responsibility. They just don't understand that I am a free spirit. Plus, I want to experience life and all the pleasures that it contains."

"And tonight, we will fill you full of pleasure." Ruby

passes Kate, sticking her hand under Kate's skirt to give a gentle squeeze to her right butt cheek.

Kate looks at the three wine glasses as Ruby flips her skirt up in the back, "So, my surprise is another woman besides you?"

"No, I invited a man to the party as it never hurts to have options. The surprise is just for you and I will personally give it to you later." Ruby meets Kate's shifting gaze with a smile.

Kate looks back towards the door as a small truck pulls into the driveway, "Sounds like fun. I am adventurous enough to not only try you, but a threesome also. Or, did you think I wouldn't"

"Oh, I knew you would. Especially after you see the hunk of man I have for tonight." Ruby walks to the front doors as Carl walks up the stairs.

"Hey," Carl lifts his hand in a sheepish wave, "I didn't know you were having other guests."

"We are only having one other guest. I want to break you out of your shell in a major way. I figure it is the only way I am going to get you to realize you want to stick with me. Consider it a motivational gift for to start the rest of our lives." Ruby steps aside to let Carl in the house.

"Um," Carl's face distorts from his brain's confusion, "You didn't need to do this. I'm not sure about this anyways."

Kate steps into the doorway, "This is a beautiful hunk of a man. Big muscles are a major turn on for me."

"Wouldn't you like to just ravage her body? I know men have a need for sexual diversity. I want to enjoy it with you while we are both single." Ruby steps behind Carl to whisper in his ear.

Kate steps back, pointing towards the wine table in the living room, "Are we going to drink?"

"Definitely. Let's enjoy a little wine before we adjourn to the bedroom for a night of fun. A toast to the good life." Ruby puts her hand on the small of Carl's back, gesturing him into the living room.

"So," Carl watches as Ruby pours three glasses of wine, "You do this often?"

Kate giggles at the thought, "Nope. Never did it before, but I have always wanted to try it. People tend to be too jealous to be this adventurous. Like this guy I know, Randy. He would never allow this to happen. But I need it. So, here I am just for the two of you to ravage me."

"I actually haven't slept with a man since the beginning of college. I figured out my beliefs back then and decided it was for the best. Men and women are different in many ways. They have different needs. I have chosen you, Carl, because I think you might be the one. So, I want to enter into the relationship with a bang and let you know what you get with me."

"Wow," Carl chugs the wine in a nervous frenzy, "I do like the idea, but I know this kind of relationship won't last. I've seen it on TV and online."

Kate sips her wine, "That was sweet, Ruby. But I don't think Carl is into this. Maybe I should just go."

"It won't be like this all the time. A one night stand is only available on the first night of our relationship. A kind of dowry if you will. Are you saying you haven't thought about this?" Ruby sets her glass down.

Ruby steps over to Kate. She lifts the front of Kate's skirt, exposing her bald puffy pussy. Ruby places her hand with fingertips just above the wet hole. She slides her hand up, fingers trailing over the clit. Kate sucks in deeply, causing Carl to shift his legs to adjust the rising pleasure in his pants. Ruby continues to slide her hand up until it reaches the V-neck of Kate's shirt. She then pulls down, exposing the large bare right breast.

Ruby begins to fondle the breast and lightly pinch the nipple. Carl sets his wine glass down with his left hand as his right hand makes a needed adjustment in his pants.

Ruby nods to Carl. Carl steps forward, hesitating for a moment as his hand sits inches away from Kate's breast. Ruby grabs his hand, pulling it the few inches needed to find its mark. Kate leans her head back onto Ruby's shoulder. Ruby pulls down on Kate's skirt causing it to fall to the hardwood floor. She spreads her legs a little farther as Ruby rubs her clit with a light touch.

"Yeah, I think this is going to be the beginning of an adventurous relationship. We should head up to the bedroom. It's the first one on the right." Ruby grabs the bottom of Kate's shirt, pulling it over her head as Carl takes her wine glass.

Kate kicks off her shoes, bolting for the stairs. Carl watches as her tits and ass bounce with every step. He looks at Ruby as if waiting for her approval.

"Is this what it is going to be like?" Carl pauses half way through his turn to the stairs.

Ruby walks past, brushing her hand from his

shoulder down his arm, "For tonight, and tonight only, cut loose. Think of her as a mobile sex toy. We can discuss our relationship after we have our fun. For the first night, the rules don't apply."

Chapter Twenty-Seven

Ruby takes Carl by the hand, leading him up the

stairs. Kate is standing in the bedroom at the foot of the

bed. Ruby releases Carl's hand. She unbuttons and unzips

her shorts, looking down as they fall to the top of the

boots. She sits on the bed, unzipping her left boot first.

Carl unbuttons his pants. He lifts his leg as he tries to pull

the jeans down, almost falling over in the process. Kate

keeps her full focus on her sexual desire kept between

Ruby's legs as she drops to her knees. Ruby kicks the

shorts off as the second boot falls to the ground. She

stands in front of Kate with the golden honeypot inches

from Kate's face hidden behind the see through lace

thong. Carl just gets his pants off as Kate leans in with her

tongue protruding from her mouth.

Ruby grasps a fistful of hair on the back of Kate's

head, stopping her, "Not yet. First, you are going to help

Carl get undressed."

Kate turns on her knees as Ruby holds her hair. Carl

stands upright, tilting his head to the side as he is unsure

of what to do. Kate reaches up, pulling down Carl's

underwear. His hardened six and a half inch throbbing

cock bobs right in Kate's face. Ruby reaches over as Carl

lifts one leg for Kate to get his clothes off. Ruby grabs the

base of Carl's manliness, bending it to line up with Kate's

mouth. Ruby pushes her head until the tip of his penis

parts her lips. Kate opens her mouth, having the large cock

inserted into her mouth as she frees the clothing from

Carl's other leg.

Ruby watches as Kate extends her neck forward to take in half of Carl. Kate slides the cock in and out with a steady tempo. Carl begins to breathe deeply with an obvious buildup of delight. Without thought or prompting, Carl reaches forward with both hands grabbing the buttoned split of Ruby's shirt. He pulls the shirt apart, letting the buttons fly. Carl grips one breast in each hand as Ruby lets slip an inviting sex noise. Ruby releases Kate's head and presses in closer to Carl. While kissing Carl, she presses her pantie covered honeypot against the back of Kate's head. Every inch of Carl's meatiness is pushed into Kate's mouth. Ruby backs up five seconds later as Kate begins to choke.

Kate looks up smiling at Ruby as her hand strokes Carl, "Is it time for my surprise?"

"Not yet, but I think I can tide you over until then," Ruby climbs onto the bed, dragging her fingertips across both of Kate's shoulders as she turns so Kate will follow.

Ruby directs Kate to lay down on the bed with her feet towards the headboard. Ruby removes her thong, throwing it at Carl. Carl steps to the foot of the bed. Ruby straddles over Kate's face. She leans back onto Carl, his hands massaging her breasts as she holds onto his neck kissing him. Kate sticks her tongue as deep inside Ruby as she can. She pulls her tongue in and out several times before dragging the tip to Ruby's clit. Kate flickers her tongue on the clit. Ruby stops kissing, looking down as she lets out another sensual sound.

Ruby arches her back, her hips swaying back and forth over Kate's tongue. She presses down, covering Kate's face with her spread pussy lips. She thrusts back and forth, face fucking Kate as she holds onto Carl with an iron grip. Ruby reaches a minor climax, thrusting her upper body forward. She breaks Carl's grip on her breasts with a wrenching motion pulling her pierced breasts apart and to the side. She lands with elbows on the bed on either side of Kate's hips. She turns part way around, running the fingers of her right hand from the small of her back down to the feminine pheromones gently secreting from her crotch. She runs her hand back up to the small of her back, leaving a wet trail behind her fingers.

Carl steps with his left leg onto the top of the wooden footboard sitting four inches lower than the mattress. Kate licks Ruby's clit with as much tongue as she can get out of her mouth. Carl, standing on the footboard, allows himself to fall to his knees on the bed with his feet still resting on the footboard. The ladies bounce around for a moment, giggling with delight. Kate grabs the base of Carl's cock, pointing it in the general direction of Ruby. Carl's hips sway forward. Kate lines him up as if aiming an arrow. The broad head finds its mark, piercing deep into Ruby. Ruby screeches with delight, swivels her head to flip her hair to the left, and gazes down upon Kate's bald puffy pussy.

Carl's first thrust goes deep. Every inch inside Ruby. He grabs ahold of her hips, holding the position for a moment as ecstasy floods over him. Kate licks from Ruby's clit to Carl's balls and back. Ruby leans in towards Kate with her head. Her tongue starts by gently touching Kate's clit and moving down, applying a little more pressure as it comes back up. Kate presses her face into Ruby's pussy, sucking on her clit as she grunts and moans. The added stimulant causes Ruby to press harder and move faster over Kate's genitals. Carl, listening to the women moan, grunt, and screech, sways his hips faster and deeper. Kate watches as his balls swing back and forth, smacking into her forehead and causing an odd amusement for her. He slams into Ruby with every inch of his manhood. Ruby stops licking to scream as she orgasms. She has dreamed of this for over a year.

Ruby leans back in, tongue pressing hard. Her left

hand grabs Kate's coinciding cheek, pulling the cheek to the side. Ruby's right hand comes around with the two fingers in the middle of her hand extended straight out. Both fingers are easily plunged to the farthest knuckle back with the lube Kate is excreting from her hole. Kate tilts her head towards Carl, opening her mouth wide and screaming with every pulsating orgasm. Carl pulls out of Ruby, pushes down on his penis, and thrusts the dripping rod into Kate's wide open mouth. Kate gags slightly as Carl thrusts in and out, his balls slapping against her eyes and nose with every inch disappearing down her throat.

Ruby slams her fingers in and out, pushing as hard as she can to penetrate deep into Kate, "Come over here, Carl. I want to see you fuck her hard."

Carl pulls out from Kate's mouth. Kate has only a moment to catch her breath before Ruby sits up, pulling Kate's legs up enough to slightly arch Kate's back. Carl kneels in front of Kate's spread legs. He leans forward, grabbing Ruby by the back of the neck. He kisses Ruby while his cock rubs against Kate.

Carl sticks the head in slowly, watching Kate squirm as she tries to get it in faster. After the head disappears into Kate, Carl slams the entire shaft in rapidly. Kate screams with pleasure. Ruby watches Carl slide in and out. Carl plays with Ruby's breasts, no longer watching himself enter Kate. Ruby presses against Kate's face, swinging her hips forwards and back. Kate closes her eyes as Ruby's loving moisture soaks her entire face.

Ruby dismounts Kate, "Carl, pull her up so she can ride you. I think it is time for her surprise."

Carl grasps hands with Kate. He pulls her up as he falls back onto the bed. Pillows stacked at the head of the bed prevent him from smacking his head open on the headboard. Kate stays on her knees, but settles down on him with a slight backwards arch. Carl and Kate moan together as he slightly parts his legs, allowing that extra inch to sink in, creating the right amount of extra pleasure.

Kate lifts herself up and down only a few inches, with both

of them enjoying the ride. Kate loses focus on Ruby as she

tilts her head back, continuing her deep penetration.

Chapter Twenty-Eight

Ruby opens the closet door. The small walk-in closet has several sexual toys and devices hanging on the racks and placed carefully on the shelves. She steps forward, knowing the exact toy she is looking for and where it sits in the closet. She lifts the toy off the hook by the belt.

Turning back towards the bed, she pauses for a moment with a smile as she watches Carl's facial expressions. She steps back into the room, lining herself up behind Kate. She grabs the dildo end of the toy, allowing the belt and straps to dangle. She lowers the toy, lifting her left leg up. She slides the other foot into the harness.

Pulling up the belt, she adjusts the belt and harness to sit properly on her body. She grabs a bottle of oil sitting on the table next to the door. She smiles as she climbs into bed behind Kate with her strap-on dildo poised for pleasure.

Ruby sets the oil down on the bed. She reaches around Kate, rubbing the back of Carl's hands as they play with Kate's breasts. Carl looks up at ruby and smiles with a mix of pleasure and romance. Ruby kisses on Kate's neck.

Ruby slides her tongue up Kate's neck, flicking Kate's earlobe before whispering, "Are you an anal virgin my dear?"

"Yes, it is an outty, not an inny. I will always get more pleasure from my pussy than my ass." Kate neither stops her hip movements, nor makes a sour face at the idea Ruby is suggesting.

Ruby slides her hands down to Kate's hips, moving with her motion, "How do you know if you haven't tried. You want a real pleasuring adventure and I want your ass. Let me show you what you really like."

"I have had more pleasure this night than ever before. You can do anything you want to me. Yes, I want you to have my ass." Kate shakes as she has another orgasm over Carl's cock, without paying much attention to her own words.

Ruby pushes Kate forward. Kate lands with both hands on the bed and her tits dangling in Carl's face. Carl opens his mouth wide, sucking in as much of her breast as he can. Ruby opens the bottle of oil, pouring from between Kate's shoulder blades all the way down to her virgin tight little anus. Carl begins to move his hips to slide in and out of Kate as the oil runs down her sides, dripping on him. Ruby pours oil over the entire shaft of the strap-on dildo.

Ruby rubs the dildo on the outside of Kate's tight little hole, only putting light pressure against the hole. With Carl still thumping in and out, Kate moans from the new sensation. Ruby inserts the realistic shaped head of the dildo in half way. She pulls it back out, rubbing against the hole once more. She inserts the head a little deeper, pulling out to rub again. When she inserts this time, the entire head almost enters.

Ruby can feel the tightness preventing her from entering completely. She pulls out till half the head is visible. The slow slide in and out only takes three thrusts until the head slips in fully. Kate moans, tightening her abs from the new fascination. Carl joins in the moan as it brings about a new sensation for him as well. Ruby slides the dildo another inch before pulling it out to the tip of the dildo. She moves her hips forward, easily sliding half of the dildo into Kate causing louder moaning to escape. Carl thrusts faster as the new sensation of tightness and textured feeling enthralls him.

Ruby slides the dildo back in with ease, this time shifting forward to sink every inch into Kate's virgin outty. Kate screams as she tightens her body. Carl grabs both of her breasts, pushing against them to hold Kate up as her arms give out from the pleasure. Ruby swings her hips forward and back in the opposite direction of Carl. Kate continues her orgasmic screaming as the multiples of orgasms flood over her. Carl closes his fingers around Kate's breasts, adding extra pressure on them. Kate's body jerks repeatedly. Ruby grabs Kate's hips, pounding the dildo deep. Every inch of the dildo disappears into Kate's ass as her cheeks spread far apart from the force of the pounding. Carl's body begins to shake as he makes new grunting and groaning noises. He pushes hard up into Kate. Ruby rams the dildo deep, holding her hips pressed against

Kate's ass. Carl screams as he squeezes harder against Kate's breasts. Kate lets out one last scream before her head drops.

Carl's body convulses as he fills Kate with his creamy white mixture deep inside her. He lowers Kate down onto his chest, allowing his arms to fall to the sides wherever they may land. He looks at Ruby as her face conveys a contented feeling. Carl smiles as the feeling of finding the one who understands the needs he never knew he had floods over him. Only his soulmate could provide such a feeling. Ruby shifts her hips, allowing the dildo to slide out of Kate's butt. Ruby looks down at Kate's anus, now puffy as her pussy.

Ruby rubs on Kate's right ass cheek, "It isn't a virgin anymore. So, was it worth it?"

"Most definitely. I never knew such pleasure." Kate mumbles from exhaustion.

Ruby pulls Carl's dick out of Kate's pussy and

strokes it, "So, did this meet all of your needs, Carl?"

"Yes," Ruby bends down, tasting both Kate and Carl as she sucks on his cock, "I have never known anything like this before. It was the best."

"Oh, is that my phone?" Kate rolls off of Carl, barely missing Ruby's head with her foot and heads to the doorway to listen for the ringer.

Ruby creates a smacking sound as she removes her mouth, "Did you have somewhere else you needed to be?"

"No, but I think I should be getting back home. It is getting late. I had the most wonderful time." Kate crosses back across the room, giving a long goodbye kiss to Ruby.

Ruby looks at the marks on Kate's breasts and the fluid covering Kate's body, "I am glad you joined us. Hope to see you around some time."

"Yeah," Carl looks as Kate walks to the doorway, "It was nice meeting you, Kate."

Ruby looks at Carl laying spread eagle on the bed,

"I think we need to shower. Are you going to stay the night with me?"

"Like you could get me to leave. But we do need to talk about things." Carl laughs at the idea of darting out the door like Kate.

Ruby stands up, beckoning Carl to join her as she approaches the bedroom door. Carl rolls out of bed. Ruby sees Kate standing in the middle of the foyer with her clothes in one hand and phone in the other. As Carl passes by, Ruby points to the bathroom in her normal bedroom.

Ruby listens as Kate's phone conversation echoes up the stairs, "I just fell asleep at my parents. I will see you in a little while. No, nothing is going on. No, you don't have to wait up for me. I will see you in the morning. Love you too."

Ruby shakes her head as she did not realize Kate would lie to her man. Ruby waves with a smile as Kate turns around to look up at her. Kate waves back, throwing on her shirt and grabbing her shoes before heading out

the door with her bare ass gleaming in the light of the

chandelier. Ruby walks around the top of the banister,

heading through the bedroom door on the left. She gets to

the oversized marble tiled bathroom just as Carl flushes

the toilet. Ruby brushes past Carl, stepping into the multi-

head shower. She adjusts the water temperature.

Chapter Twenty-Nine

Carl comes up behind her, wrapping both arms around her stomach and pressing his softening penis into her butt, "Are you an anal virgin my dear?"

"Although it has been played with by myself and a few women, I am an anal virgin because it has never been touched by the hands of man or his cock. If all goes well, it will be yours and yours alone." Ruby giggles at Carl's cute quote.

Carl kisses on Ruby's neck as the showerheads

shoot the steamy water over their bodies. The mixture of sweat, oil, and bodily fluids runs down to the tile below. After they each wash their own hair, the couple take turns washing each other clean. The time is fun for both, but they both get a sense of romance rather than a continuation of sex. Getting out of the shower and drying off, Ruby sighs a heavy sigh of contentment as she is filled with a feeling of choosing her mate wisely.

Ruby follows Carl to the bed, laying her head on the top of his outstretched arm, "I know this relationship is on the right path for me. So, do you think this relationship could work for you Carl?"

"I do have to admit I am a little fuzzy on what this relationship is, but that isn't to say I am not interested in you. It is hard to say if it can work if you don't really know what it is." Carl brings his hand around, laying it softly on Ruby's breast.

Ruby places her hand on top of his, "Well, this is

how I think it should work. We take some time to get to know each other. Not only what each other likes, but what our core beliefs are. It will be important to make sure we have a solid base for the long term or children. We need to make sure we are right for one another."

"We have gotten to know each other over the last two years to a certain degree. I agree we have more to learn. Although the relationship will have lots of sex, I am afraid it can't be all we have." Carl shifts his left leg.

Ruby rubs on the back of his hand, "True, but I mean we really get to know each other. I have had feelings for you for a long time now. I am hoping we will one day get married. On that day, I will no longer be an anal virgin."

"Okay. Not sure about that, but to be honest, I have had feelings for you also. Although, I really don't know how to say this, but I would need to know how the sex would work. It seems confusing with what you say you believe and what you bring into the relationship."

Ruby looks up at Carl, "You mean having others join in? It was nice for us to do that as we come together, but there are rules which we have to set in place for this and agree upon. We have to follow what we believe for the rules. We have to know we will not break the rules. And, no more partners until we get married."

"I can agree to that," Carl pulls gently on Ruby's piercing, "But, are you going to want to bring in other men?"

Ruby looks down, placing her hand on the inside of his leg, "Do you swing that way? Cause, two things, we have to be honest and there can't be any other men."

"No, I don't want any man. I was just thinking if we brought other women into the relationship, then you might also want other men. Fair is fair, I suppose." Carl glances around the room as the hope of Ruby not thinking it is fair fills his mind.

Ruby rubs her hand up and down his leg, "No, there can only be one man per house. Think of it this way. Once we get married, we become one. As one, we will be dating other women. They will stay with us and we will be their only sex partners. Being a therapist, I know men have several needs when it comes to sex. I may know a lot about sex, but I am not able to give everything to you in a single package. Tell me what kinds of women you find attractive."

"Well," Carl hesitates as this conversation is becoming even odder for a first serious talk, "I actually like long hair. I like their bodies to be hairless below their head. I like piercings, but if the breasts are large enough, then I guess it doesn't really matter. Stuff like that?"

Ruby runs her hand up onto his limp penis, "Yes, just like that, but more. You don't have to come up with the entire list today. We will figure out what you want in body type like you described, and what things you like to do to a woman. Maybe things are different based on what kind of day you are having. But to make the point, I don't have extremely large breasts. Us dating other women gives the option for you to have everything you need to be totally satisfied. Plus, I do like to swing both ways. I don't think your hard pecks are going to do much for me when I want to suckle on a pair of breasts. And if I am in the mood to lick a little twat, you are no help at all. If we are both satisfied with each other, and we have the needs met we cannot supply to each other, our love will flourish."

"You are an odd lady, but I am glad you like me. I do have one request. My mom has been given nine months to live. Is it possible we will get married before then so she can be there?" Carl's hand slides to the side of Ruby's breast as he tightens his shoulders.

Ruby grabs his hand, wrapping his arm around to place it on her other breast, "It can happen. It means we would have to work hard at the relationship to find our true compatibility. We do need to be sure there won't be problems. Nine months isn't a long time, but if we are honest from the start, it might work out for us. I don't want to get divorced like many who don't do marriage right."

Carl relaxes as Ruby tilts her head into his chest. He watches Ruby close her eyes. He stares at the wall wondering what all will be involved in this strangely awesome relationship. Although he has had loose beliefs in the past, this seems like a new way to approach beliefs he has had tucked away. He slowly closes his eyes as he ponders the things to come.

Chapter Thirty

Abigail stirs. Her arm flies over to the alarm off button. Her head lifts a mere inch off the pillow. Her eyes pop open. The cover is flung off exposing her body to the air and the new day. She winces as she struggles to climb out of bed. Her nipples feel like someone smashed them with a sludge hammer and her crotch was pounded by a jack hammer. Even with the pain, she could not be stopped. She rushed into the living room. Her head bounces back and forth as the love song returns to blast in her head. She spies her cell phone sitting on the table. She walks over scooping it into her hand pushing the home button. She swipes the screen. Her face drops with her left hand forming a fist and magically finding its way onto her hip. Randy had not called or texted to get coffee.

"Maybe he is just going to meet me down there," Abigail states setting the phone down on the table, "I should get ready and meet him down at the coffee shop."

Abigail looks out the window on the opposite side of the table. She tilts her head as a wide eyed twelve year old boy sits in the apartment building across the alley staring at her. Her face scrunches as she wonders why he looks so surprised and yet extremely excited. She looks down realizing she has no clothes on to cover her naked body. Her eyes widen as she realizes the boy not only has the perfect view of her breasts and nipples, but her hairy pussy sits about an inch above her discount table.

Abigail covers her breasts with her right forearm

and hand and averts the view of her crotch with her other

hand. She spins on the ball of her left foot and runs for the

bedroom. The door slams shut with her bare skin pressing

against it. It takes almost two minutes for the

embarrassment to wear off before she can remove herself

from the door. She takes a step forward before stopping.

Abigail looks down gently cupping the bottoms of

her breasts, "Sorry boy, these girls are only for Randy. And,

it is time for them to go see their prince."

Abigail laughs as she rummages through her

clothing. She wants to pick out a nice outfit for her

morning coffee date. As she fixes her white brief panties,

she pulls them away from her waist to take a look at her

bruised hairy crotch as if she might figure out a way to

make it hurt less. She adjusts her wireless full coverage bra

several times before deciding there is no good position for

her bruised breasts and nipples. They will hurt no matter

what she does. She decides the blue skirt would be a

better than the jeans she picked out. Although they give a nice curve to her rear, the pain of the crotch is not worth it.

Abigail grabs a light purple short sleeve t-shirt off the bed. She pulls it down just before opening the bedroom door. She crosses over to the bathroom. It seems to take forever to empty her bladder as she impatiently waits to leave. She washes her hands, briefly taking a moment to brush her hair before turning to the bathroom door. She scrunches her face as she stares at the open door. Has love affected her so much she is open for anything?

She walks into the living room to find the boy still in the window. But this time, the boy is not alone. His mother is standing facing him. The mother is pointing at a giant drool smear on the window as if a dog's face rubbed against the glass. Abigail's eyes widen and mouth opens slightly realizing the boy had drooled on the window watching her, or at least she hopes it is drool. The mother

begins to turn towards the window.

Abigail freaks while trying to grab her school bag

and run out the door before the mother sees her and

figures out what happened. The door slams shut behind

her. She freezes in the hallway to make sure no one

noticed. She looks up and down the hall. She looks up to

the ceiling wishing Randy would walk around the corner to

cure her embarrassment.

But, Randy cannot be here if he is meeting her at

the coffee shop. Abigail takes a deep breath. She makes a

beeline for the stairs. The front door flies open making a

chinking metal sound as it is over extended. Abigail races

through the streets to get to the coffee shop. She blurs out

everyone she passes. The only thing of importance is to

get to the brew house. She gets to the street corner on the

same block as the coffee shop.

Abigail pauses with the door now in sight. The

church bells a couple blocks over makes her tilt her head. She turns back towards the bank she passed on the last block. The electronic sign says only seven thirty. She laughs at all the stress she was under to get here. She is half an hour early. Plenty of time to settle down before meeting up with Randy. She will even have time to tell Tonya about her magical prince and the adventure he took her on last night.

Abigail turns towards the coffee shop with a sway in her step. As she steps in front of the barber shop, she stops dead in her tracks. She watches as Randy opens the door to the coffee shop from inside. Abigail's smile disappears as he holds the door open for the woman she met at the grocery store. The woman is wearing the same clothes she had on the day before, just in different colors. Randy puts his hand on the small of the woman's back as they walk straight for Abigail. Randy looks through Abigail as if he does not know her.

Randy starts to guide the woman around Abigail before she sidesteps causing them both to look at Abigail, "Hello Randy."

"Hello Abigail," Randy looks innocently with a smile as if just realizing who she is, "How are you today?"

"Oh, Hello. Remember me from the grocery store? Kate." Kate giggles putting her right arm behind Randy, leaning on him kicking one leg off the ground at her knee.

"Yes, I remember you," Abigail looks over at Kate briefly before returning her gaze to Randy, "I thought you were going to call so we could meet for coffee this morning?"

Kate laughs as she lets go of Randy and straightens up, "Yeah, funny how small this town really seems, as big as it really is. We have run into four of Randy's old flames since we got here a week ago. You all seem intent on winning him over, but I am afraid he is taken as of this morning's coffee."

Kate holds out her right hand separating her other fingers to make the ring finger stand alone. The diamond ring on her finger is not overly gaudy, but is not small either. Abigail slowly draws in her breath while staring at the ring. Kate's small leather purse slips off her other shoulder onto the sidewalk just behind her. She whips around to face the purse. Abigail continues to stare as if the ring is still visible.

Kate stands feet shoulder width apart bending over at the waist. Her micro skirt rides a little over half way up her ass. Abigail refocuses realizing Kate has on no underwear. Abigail has a perfect view of Kate's shaved pussy, large clit, and puffy hard ridden anus. Kate's shirt billows down at the waist. She is still not wearing a bra giving Abigail the back drop of her tits swaying behind and just below her pussy. Abigail continues to stare as if a piece of art creating an arousal in her down deep.

"Gotta love that," Randy attracts the attention of

both women.

Kate turns her head to look at Randy first, then Abigail without standing up, "Liking what you see? I can't blame you for enjoying the view. Of course, maybe it isn't Randy you are pining over."

Kate stands up, turning towards Abigail swinging her arm in-between Randy's body and outstretched arm. She pulls his arm in close positioning his hand left at her crotch. Randy gives a perverted smile as he grasps a handful of puffy bald pussy through the skirt with his fingertips curling into the wetness behind the skirt. Abigail stands speechless breathing slowly. Kate nudges Randy to the side to begin walking around Abigail.

Randy looks over towards Abigail, "See you around someday."

Kate looks back as Abigail turns to look at her, "You'll find the right girl for you one day."

Kate flips her skirt up in the back showing her bare

ass to Abigail and everyone else on the street. Abigail turns quickly towards the coffee shop, unsure if she is feeling sadness or rage. Moving on full autopilot, Abigail forces the heavy door open. She continues her way to the front counter. She blankly watches as Tonya walks up to the register. Tonya stands for a moment watching Abigail stare at her chest. Abigail brings her eyes up, lightly swollen and filled with unmoving tears. As Abigail makes eye contact, the tears begin to flow with gentle sobs. Abigail brings both hands up to her mouth as she cries.

Tonya turns to the other barista, "I am going to need a few minutes. Can you make an amaretto cream latte, please?"

The other barista nods watching the public display of emotion. Tonya quickly moves around the counter putting one arm around Abigail with her other hand on the opposite shoulder. Tonya guides Abigail to the far corner booth away from the majority of prying eyes. Abigail slides into the booth with Tonya following her.

Abigail sobs as she looks deep into Tonya's eyes, "Why don't you hate me? I was so mean. I should have believed you. He just seemed so innocent like me."

"I know it's tough when someone steals your innocence. But, you will get through this. I know this will help you in the long run. Now you can focus on you without worrying about finding someone else. This isn't the end, it is just a bumpy rapids. Time will heal you and guide you to the one you are meant to be with in the future." Tonya reaches up placing her hand softly on Abigail's cheek.

Abigail nods twice. Her chin begins to quiver as the waterworks flow stronger. She throws her arms around Tonya's lower body as she buries her face in Tonya's large chest. Tonya's chest muffles the sounds from Abigail's crying. Tonya puts one arm around her back and strokes her hair with the other. They sit for five minutes oblivious to the other customers around them, or those who are

coming and going. Abigail finally stops crying so forcefully.

"You know, this would be great for me if it wasn't

so sad for you," Tonya looks down at Abigail as Abigail

looks up feeling the breasts shift slightly after five minutes.

Tonya gives a gentle smile while raising her

eyebrows up and down a few times in quick secession.

Tonya looks from Abigail's head to her own breasts and

back a few times until Abigail realizes what Tonya means.

Abigail stops sobbing and her tears slow to a stop. She

turns her head to put the side of her face against Tonya's

breasts.

"It might be," Abigail still has a tremor in her voice,

"If you didn't have on so many clothes, and if you didn't

smell like a caramel mocha latte."

Tonya laughs quietly. Her hand continues to stroke

Abigail's hair. Abigail sighs the heavy sigh of comfort

needed after any life wrenching event. The door chime

sounds as another guest enters the shop. Tonya and

Abigail both look at the new comer.

Chapter Thirty-One

Ruby opens her eyes, looking at the alarm clock. Six thirty in the morning. She can feel Carl's hardened meat pressed lightly against her ass as they lay spooning. She smiles as she shifts her hips up to wake him. As she slides her hips back down, she exclaims the feeling of pain suddenly jarring the hole she wasn't aiming for.

Carl raises his head, propping onto his right arm, "What? What's wrong?"

"Nothing, I just got stabbed by a sharp stick in the

butt," Ruby's voice quivers with irritation as the move killed her mood.

Carl reaches over, placing his hand on her stomach, "I thought we were waiting for that. It is nice to see you. I could get use to waking up to this sight every morning."

"And so you shall, my hunk of love," Ruby turns her head as Carl's hand runs from her stomach up to cup her breasts.

Carl looks at the clock and groans, "Sadly, I don't have time to appreciate this fully. I need to be at the hospital in an hour to finalize the paperwork and get my mom. Will you be stopping by the gym today?"

"Not today, but maybe we can get together after your shift," Ruby pushes her hips against Carl one last time before rolling out of the elegant bed.

Carl smiles as he rolls the opposite way, "I would like that. I can call you after I get my mom settled in, or on my lunch break. We can see how busy your schedule will be."

"I will make time for you. But tell me, will you always be this happy to see me in the mornings?" Ruby glances down at the little man standing fully erect.

Carl looks down at Ruby's breasts, "If you take care of his needs, he will always be happy to see you. I need a bathroom and clothes. I have got to get there before the hospital causes problems."

Carl walks around the bed, kissing Ruby while placing one hand on the small of her back. Ruby watches as Carl heads for the bathroom. She follows behind him a moment later. She watches as Carl carefully aims with his enlarged weapon. She grins as she notices him watching her out of the corner of his eye.

As Carl finishes and walks towards the door, Ruby stops him for one last kiss. Her left hand grabs onto the shrinking penis. She gently pulls as the kiss ends and he finishes walking out of the room. Ruby walks over, tipping the seat to let it fall flat. The seat, which she had never

lifted before, slowed half way down. Ruby sits just as the

seat touches the rim. She watches through the door as

Carl walks back and forth to find all of his scattered

clothing. She turns to grab a few squares of toilet paper.

Ruby turns back around to find Carl is standing in

the doorway, "Need a hand before I go?"

"No, I can handle it today. I don't want to make you

late. Maybe some other time. You gonna tell your mom

about me?" Ruby chuckles at the thought of Carl licking

her clean.

Carl taps on the door frame twice, "I sure will. Talk

to you in a little while."

"Bye," Ruby spreads her legs and wipes.

Ruby walks into the closet, rotating in the closet as

she thinks about clothes for the day. As she has a meeting

with higher echelon clients, she decides to go with black

dress crop pants and a somewhat revealing lightweight

dressy black shirt. Of course, she is going with a thong as she eithers wears those or nothing at all. Having dressed, Ruby heads out the door, piling into the car. She looks at the back seat with a smile. Her puppy is coming home today.

Ruby drives downtown towards the appointment. As she approaches the area she had the appointment in yesterday, she pulls over to park in the same spot. The lady who gave her dirty looks yesterday gives a little wave and a quiet hello as if she doesn't recognize Ruby with her shirt on. Ruby half grins with a wave. Ruby crosses the quiet street.

With the idea of a pleasant morning, Ruby walks to the coffee shop door. She has enough time to get a specialty cup before going to her appointment. She swings the door open wide. As she steps in the laser triggers a chime. Two ladies sitting in the corner look up at her. Ruby feels bad for the one who looks to have been crying, but cannot spare the time today to help.

Ruby walks to the front counter, examining the menu for a moment before ordering a super double deluxe chocolate latte. She glances over at the two ladies as the one crying lays her head back on the barista's large breasts. Ruby feels a sense of relief as she is not needed. The latte is set on the counter, drawing Ruby's attention back to her day. She pays for the drink, moving a small two person booth on the far wall.

Just as she sits and puts her leg up, the door chimes. Ruby recognizes the woman she ran into yesterday. She smiles as her attention returns to her chocolate.

Chapter Thirty-Two

Jill wakes to find John looking at her as the light crests into the room. She is still laying on his chest with his hand on her breast. She realizes her hand is laying on top of his penis, or rather extremely hard cock. She wraps her fingers around the large rod with a gentle, slow jerking motion. John begins to breathe deeply. Jill looks up at him raising her eyebrows twice in rapid succession.

Jill turns over on her side, lifting her leg and using her hand to spread her butt cheeks, "Would you like a morning quickie?"

"I would never pass up the chance with you. I guess this means you don't want it to be a one night thing." John slides down in the bed.

Jill begins to rub her left nipple with her right hand, "Definitely not. But not at work anymore unless the front door is locked or we are locked in the back office. What would you say if I said I wanted Tonya to join in with us sometime?"

John uses his hand to wiggle the head around to lubricate the rim of the hole so he can slide in, "I agree about the work. Would be weird with a client walking in on us. The Tonya thing depends on what you mean by it."

Jill sighs as the cock slides in for her early morning wakeup call, "I'm not sure. The more I think about it, the more exciting it was being watched."

John begins to move faster. Jill pulls harder to spread her cheeks just a little further. She tilts her head towards the pillow as John reaches around grabbing her stomach. He slams in hard, holding the position as he grunts. His entire body relaxes as his head falls to the pillow next to her. He rubs on her belly with a sigh of contentment.

"I noticed you didn't cum. Did you want me to help you finish?" John stares at the back of Jill's head, "And, are you going into the office today as scheduled?"

Jill turns her upper body so she can see John, "No dear. This morning was all for you. I won't be in the office today because Kyle is coming home from camp. If I don't get his clothes into the wash right away, he will stink up our entire house. But, what did you mean by what I mean by the Tonya thing?"

"First, I think Tonya might be a lesbian, which would ruin things for sex. But, you need to decide if you want it to go forward, and what you want out of it. You know I think that since we are married we are one. We could have Tonya or another woman as a concubine, but

that would open up several doors and situations you might

not have thought through. It would mean we would both

be having sex with her. You just need to think it over

before you commit." John sighs a little less comfortably

with the conversation taking a serious tone.

Jill slides off the bed heading for the bathroom, "I

will think it through. I know we have discussed the idea

and what you think before, but maybe we can go over it

again tonight. I am actually serious this time."

"Sure thing. I will see you after work. What are we

having for dinner?" John rolls out of the bed.

Jill waits until exiting the bathroom before

answering, "Thought we might do pot roast with carrots

and potatoes."

"Sound good. Love you." John enters the bathroom

and flips on the water for a shower.

Jill grabs her tote, tossing it on the bed, "Love you."

Jill pulls a change of clothes out of the tote. She dresses with the occasional glance in the mirror. She looks in the mirror after being fully dressed. After a moment, she sighs a content sigh as her life has opened to a new chapter. She collects her things together in the tote. She looks down at her feet seeing the light dance off of a piece of plastic. She bends down grabbing the plastic bag, realizing it is the nipple clamps. She smiles with thoughts of tomorrow in her head.

Jill walks by the bathroom door on her way out. She giggles at the sound of her husband singing off key in the shower. She hollers a goodbye. She takes little notice of anyone else in the hotel or parking lot as she walks to the minivan. After throwing her tote in the middle seat and climbing into the driver's seat, she looks up at someone walking in front of the van. She smiles as she recognizes the young woman who got a free peep show. The young woman looks down at the pavement as she realizes Jill is observing her, walking faster as she tries to

escape the embarrassment.

Jill laughs softly as the minivan sputters to life. Jill

winds through the streets towards her home. She cuts

down a side street heading out of her way. Jill pulls the van

over, parking by the curb. She gets out and looks across

the street at the little coffee shop. A strange grin appears

on her face as she heads towards the front door. She pulls

the door open. The chime sounds as she enters letting

everyone know she has arrived.

The redhead who bumped into her is sitting on one

side of the coffee shop. The lady looks up briefly at Jill.

Tonya and a lady nestled on her bosom look up for a

moment. Jill waves to Tonya. Tonya returns the gesture

with a free hand. Jill realizes her husband was right, Tonya

might be a lesbian. Jill snickers to herself as she walks to

the front counter to order a drink.

Jude Lawson

The sun radiates down upon all those walking in the masses of the street in front of The Little Columbian Coffee Shoppe. The weather woman is guaranteeing rain for the afternoon, but this morning will be the beautiful start for a new day. With the mysteries of love, romance, and sex floating on a warm summer breeze. The lives of three women, seemingly unconnected, advance one more day as life goes through the excitement of rallying another night to come.

Thank you for your patronage.

You can find other books at:

www.pagodaswap.website

Merchandise is also available.

Don't forget, we appreciate your

feedback on Amazon & Createspace.

www.ingramcontent.com/pod-product-compliance
Lightning Source LLC
Chambersburg PA
CBHW051413170626
46809CB00006B/2149